Michael Underwood and The Murder Room

>>> This title is part of The Murder Room, our series dedicated to making available out-of-print or hard-to-find titles by classic crime writers.

Crime fiction has always held up a mirror to society. The Victorians were fascinated by sensational murder and the emerging science of detection; now we are obsessed with the forensic detail of violent death. And no other genre has so captivated and enthralled readers.

Vast troves of classic crime writing have for a long time been unavailable to all but the most dedicated frequenters of second-hand bookshops. The advent of digital publishing means that we are now able to bring you the backlists of a huge range of titles by classic and contemporary crime writers, some of which have been out of print for decades.

From the genteel amateur private eyes of the Golden Age and the femmes fatales of pulp fiction, to the morally ambiguous hard-boiled detectives of mid twentieth-century America and their descendants who walk our twenty-first century streets, The Murder Room has it all. **>>>**

The Murder Room
Where Criminal Minds Meet

themurderroom.com

Michael Underwood (1916–1992)

Michael Underwood (the pseudonym of John Michael Evelyn) was born in Worthing, Sussex and educated at Christ Church College, Oxford. He was called to the Bar in 1939 and served in the British army during World War Two. He returned to work in the Department of Public Prosecutions until his retirement in 1976, and wrote almost 50 crime novels informed by his career in the law. His five series characters include Sergeant Nick Atwell and lawyer Rosa Epton, of whom is was said by the *Washington Post* that she 'outdoes Perry Mason'.

By Michael Underwood

Girl Found Dead

Michael Underwood

An Orion book

Copyright © Isobel Mackenzie 1963

The right of Michael Underwood to be identified as the author of this
work has been asserted in accordance with the Copyright, Designs and
Patents Act 1988.

This edition published by
The Orion Publishing Group Ltd
Orion House
5 Upper St Martin's Lane
London WC2H 9EA

An Hachette UK company
A CIP catalogue record for this book is available from the British Library

ISBN 978 1 4719 0784 5

www.orionbooks.co.uk

For Mary Thompson

CHAPTER ONE

Immediately his eyes opened, George Andrews knew what had woken him. It was the landing light shining beneath the bedroom door feebly etching its warped contours. Beside him his wife stirred. He could tell that she had been waiting for him to wake up and knew before she spoke what her first words would be.

'Are you awake, dear?' Her tone was timidly reproachful and he answered her with a grunt while he fought to check the feeling of exasperation she so readily aroused in him.

'The landing light's still on,' she continued in an anxious whisper. 'Something must have happened to Susan. It's after two o'clock and she promised she'd be home by midnight.'

'She's probably in bed and just forgot to switch it off.'

'She's never forgotten before. Do you think you'd better . . .'

George Andrews gave a long-suffering sigh. 'Yes, all right, I'll go and see.' He swung his legs out of bed and felt for his slippers.

'Why don't you turn on the light, dear?'

He swallowed the comment which came to his lips, and, groping his way across to the door, found the switch. He peered about him with bleary eyes, watched anxiously by his wife.

'Where's my dressing-gown? It's blasted cold out of bed.' He threw his wife a resentful glance. 'And stop fussing, Winnie. I tell you Susan's probably tucked up in bed. I'll give her a good bawling out in the morning, leaving lights burning like that. She can make a contribution out of her pocket money next time the electricity bill comes in.'

Winnie Andrews, lying white-faced and tense and irritatingly submissive, said nothing. To think that this was the same shy, attractive girl he had married twenty-five years ago when he had been an alert young constable in the county force. Much had happened in those twenty-five years, though, unhappily, little which had seen fulfilment of any of their original dreams. They had even had to wait nine years for Susan to be born and then been denied the hope of any further children.

The trouble had been, George Andrews now reflected as he stared at his wife's recumbent form, that she had never been cut out to be a policeman's wife. What better evidence was there on that than the fact of his premature retirement on her account? She hadn't liked being left alone at nights when he was out on a case and had always carped in her quietly plaintive way about the irregular hours. The shy girl of twenty-five years ago had turned into a neurotic woman. Thank goodness Susan seemed to take after him rather than her mother. She was as healthy a sixteen-year-old as you could hope to meet, and a good deal less trouble than many of her age.

He opened the bedroom door and pattered across the landing. Susan's door was shut and he turned the handle very quietly. That was one thing he'd learnt to do in the police: open doors quietly. The room was dark inside and he paused to listen for sounds of breathing. There were none. He put out a hand and touched the edge of the pillow. It was cold. A second later he had switched on the light and confirmed that the room was empty.

'She hasn't come in yet,' he announced bleakly as he returned to the other bedroom.

His wife gave a little cry. 'I knew something awful had happened to her. What are we going to do?'

'First thing to do is to stop your imagination running wild. Nothing may have happened to her at all. Certainly none of the things you're thinking of.'

'Then why isn't she home? Where on earth can she be at this hour of the night?'

'She may have decided to spend the night at Christine's.'

'But why?'

'I don't know,' he said grimly. 'But I'll soon find out.' He moved over to the chair on which his clothes lay folded. 'I thought this was a school dance she was going to.'

'It was. She was to pick up Christine and they were going on together. She said it finished at half-past eleven and she promised she'd be in by midnight.'

George Andrews said nothing further as he quickly slipped on his clothes. He was, however, beginning to feel as worried as his wife.

'Are you going to ring the police?'

'No.' Then, observing her expression, he added, 'There's no point in phoning the police yet—not until I've been round to Christine Thrupp's house and found out what's happened. If the police knew anything, they'd have been on to us.'

His wife gave a distracted nod and suddenly got out of bed. He knew that she was unconvinced that he was doing the right thing, but then if she had her way, she'd not only be telephoning the police but arranging to have the church bells rung as well.

'Now what are you going to do?' he asked in a gritty tone.

'Perhaps I should come with you to the Thrupps'.' As a petulant afterthought, she added, 'I don't know why they're not on the telephone.'

'It'd be better if you stayed here,' he said firmly. 'You can put on the kettle and make some tea. I'll need a hot drink by the time I get back.'

'How long will you be gone?'

'Five minutes there, five minutes back and a couple of minutes to find out if Christine knows where our Susan is.'

The Thrupps lived about a mile and a half from the Andrewses, and Christine, who was a few months younger than Susan, had been her inseparable friend since they'd first met at school. But that represented the only link between the two families, who otherwise had little in common. Christine's father was one of Society's pricklier thorns, anti- almost everything and in particular anti-authority as spelt with a capital A.

As he reversed the Ford Anglia out of the garage, George Andrews's expression was grim. If anything *had* happened to Susan, he wouldn't rest till justice had been done. And that meant justice as he recognised it. Since his retirement from the police four years before, Susan had become the repository of his few remaining hopes.

Though he was earning more money now than he had as a detective-inspector, he still felt bitter over the circumstances which had precipitated his retirement, a bitterness which was aggravated by the private knowledge that he had failed to earn either the esteem or the affection of his colleagues. Now, as a security officer at Yander's Radio and Television Factory, he didn't bother whether anyone liked him or not.

He drew up outside the Thrupps' house and strode purposefully up to the front door. There was not a sign of life anywhere, though this was scarcely surprising at half past two in the morning. He set about rousing someone.

He had given the door a third heavy pounding when he noticed the furtive pulling aside of a curtain at one of the upstairs windows. Expecting such a move, he had stepped back from the door between each assault so that he would be visible to anyone reconnoitring the cause of all the disturbance. A moon was shining fitfully through gaps in a bank of low cloud and its light was sufficient for recognising general outlines and shapes. A few seconds later the window was opened and Thrupp's head and shoulders appeared. 'Who's there?'

'It's George Andrews, Mr. Thrupp.'

'What do you want?' The tone was suspicious and Andrews was tempted to reply sarcastically that he was no longer with the police and that Thrupp therefore had nothing to worry about.

'I'd like to speak to you urgently. It's about my daughter, I'm afraid something may have happened to her.'

The window was noisily closed, and a minute or two later Thrupp appeared at the front door dressed in an old khaki shirt, long woollen underpants and a pair of laceless gym shoes. All relics of an army career spent largely in detention barracks.

'Is your daughter home?'

'What, Christine?'

Andrews nodded quickly.

'She came in around half-eleven. Why? What's up?'

'Susan hasn't come in yet and they went to the dance at the school together.'

'Well, Christine's in all right,' Thrupp said defensively.

'I'd like to speak to her myself for a moment. Could you fetch her?' Thrupp appeared to be sourly weighing this request when Andrews went on, 'She'll probably know where Susan went after the dance. Mrs. Andrews and I are very worried over what can have happened to her.' He paused and gave Thrupp a flicker of a placatory smile. 'After all, I don't knock people up at half-past two in the morning just for fun.'

Leaving him standing on the doorstep, Thrupp disappeared inside the dark house. George Andrews waited with growing impatience for what seemed like eternity, and was on the point of pushing his way inside when the door opened and he could see Christine standing just behind her father. He called her name and she shuffled forward and greeted him with a cavernous yawn.

'Hello, Mr. Andrews,' she said, trying to stifle the yawn and at the same time hugging an

7

out-grown dressing-gown to her which made her pyjama-ed legs look unnecessarily functional.

'Do you know what's happened to Susan?' he asked urgently, and immediately thought he detected a certain wariness in her manner.

'No.' She shook her head in open-eyed innocence. 'Isn't she home then?'

She was suddenly very wide awake, which George Andrews found curiously disquieting. 'What time did you last see her?'

The girl bit her lip and appeared thoughtful. 'I can't really remember, Mr. Andrews.'

'Did you leave the dance together?'

She shuffled her feet uncomfortably. 'No. Well, not exactly.'

'Do you mean that Susan left before you did?'

'Yes, that's right. She left a bit before I did.'

'With someone?'

'I didn't notice.'

George Andrews knew that it would be fatal to show his irritation at her deliberate obtuseness. With a supreme effort at patience, he said, 'I know you don't wish to get Susan into trouble, but you must understand how worried Mrs. Andrews and I are about her. So please tell me everything that happened. For Susan's sake you must tell me, Christine. Now, who was it you saw her leave the dance with?'

'I didn't see her leave the dance with anyone.

Honestly I didn't, Mr. Andrews.'

She seemed on the verge of tears as he went on, 'What did she say to you before she left? She must have told you why she was going.'

'She didn't.'

'You mean that she didn't speak to you at all before she left?' He looked at her reproachfully. 'That's not true, is it, Christine?'

'I just thought she was going home. I think she said she had a headache.'

'What time was that?'

'Near the end.'

'Were you together the whole evening?' The girl hesitated, and he added, 'You must tell me more than you have, Christine.' She was now staring at him in open-eyed bewilderment. 'It's half-past two in the morning and Susan's not come home. Something awful may have happened to her. You must help me.'

With a great choking sob, Christine suddenly turned and buried her face in her father's side. 'I don't know where she is. I promise you I don't,' she stammered through her tears.

'But you do know something you haven't told me, don't you?' he urged.

'No . . . no . . . oh, no.'

'Then it'll be for the police to find out.'

'Don't you start threatening my daughter,' Thrupp broke in belligerently. 'It's not Christine's fault if your Susan doesn't come home at a proper hour. You want to be careful

9

before you start accusing people of things.'

George Andrews's shoulders sagged as he said wearily, 'I wasn't blaming Christine or accusing anyone of anything.' He turned to go. 'If you do remember anything else, Christine, let me know at once, won't you?'

Leaving the girl still weeping against her father's sleeve, he walked slowly back to his car. On an impulse he decided to drive home past Yander's factory where he worked. It meant going two or three miles out of his way, but there was just a chance that one of the night watchmen, all of whom knew Susan, had seen her in the course of the evening.

As he approached, his car headlights illuminated the stout wire fence which surrounded the factory. At night one had the impression that some sinister secret organisation must be in possession of the place, and George Andrews reflected with grim satisfaction that there had been no burglarious entries since he had taken over as security officer. As the car drew up with its bonnet almost nuzzling the main gate, he flicked his lights off and on to attract attention, and called out his name as soon as one of the two guards emerged from the small brick building at the side of the main entrance. Bowyer, the guard in question, appeared nonplussed at seeing his chief at such an hour, but immediately assumed it was part of a security exercise.

'All quiet, Mr. Andrews. Nothing to report. I've just done a round and Gale is patrolling now.'

'I haven't come about that. I wondered whether either of you might have seen my daughter this evening. She went to a dance at the school and hasn't come home.'

Bowyer looked shocked. 'No, I haven't seen a soul, Mr. Andrews. And I'm sure Gale would have told me if he had.' He shook her head slowly. 'That's worrying, isn't it!'

'It was just an outside chance you might have seen her.' Before the guard could say anything further, Andrews had got back into the car and driven off. His return journey through the silent village street was accompanied by only the deepest foreboding. No one knew better than he, an ex-police officer, the perils which could befall a girl of sixteen, particularly when she was as healthily attractive as Susan. On the other hand he comforted himself with the thought that she had never shown the sort of precocity with boys which inevitably spelt trouble. Moreover, though she was only of average build, she was physically fit and surprisingly strong, having always enjoyed the games side of school life more than most girls of her age. He could not imagine her succumbing easily to the first Ted who might accost her. This last thought, however, brought him mixed solace since the greater the struggle she might put up, the more vicious her assailant might become.

As he drove, his eyes searched every doorway, every turning in the hope that he might suddenly catch sight of her. He shivered when he thought of the absolute maze of footpaths and lanes which formed a web round the village of Offing. Along any one of them Susan might at this moment be stumbling, physically violated and mentally shocked into incoherence. Worse, she might still be lying bruised and unconscious in the corner of a field, even be dead—Susan, who only a few hours before had set out from home brimful of health. George Andrews winced as he recalled how she had obviously taken special trouble over her appearance that evening and how he had taken her to task when she had looked in to bid her mother and him good night.

'Come here a minute, Susan. Yes, I thought so, you're wearing too much make-up. You don't need stuff on your eyelids at your age. Just go easy with the muck next time.'

She had coloured up and pouted her annoyance at his tone. 'If Mum doesn't mind, I don't see why you should,' she had replied over her shoulder, and then quickly gone out before either of her parents had been able to speak.

He wondered if it were possible that she was still in a pique at being told off and was deliberately frightening her parents by staying out late in order to teach them a lesson. It seemed incredible, though she had on a few rare occasions reacted unpredictably to rebukes. She was not by any means a hyper-sensitive girl, but when her vanity was wounded she could become as capricious as any mule on a mountain pass.

George Andrews swallowed hard at his recollection of the sharpness of their parting that evening, for he knew that Susan deep down was as fond of him as he was proud of her. Between them lay a bond of steady affection which was not repeated between daughter and mother. Not that Winnie didn't love Susan, she did. But it was a love so inhibited by fuss that it manifested itself in a never-ceasing flow of anxious inquiry and wild imaginings which left little room for understanding.

His mind tacked away on a new course as he tried to recall the names of boys he had heard Susan mention of late. The trouble had always been that as soon as he had committed one name to memory sufficiently well to make an interested inquiry after its bearer, he would invariably be met with some such scornful reply as, 'Oh, him! I haven't seen him for ages.'

There had, of course, been that young fellow, Michael Neale, whom she had met at the church fête last summer. His mother, Lady Neale, had opened it and Susan and Christine had been there to give a hand at one of the stalls. Susan had obviously been flattered by young Neale's attention—he was up at Cambridge and moved in far more sophisticated circles than any other boys she knew—but on the other hand she had made little protest when at an early stage her father had discouraged the possibility of a friendship developing. It was not that he wished to restrict her social horizon. Indeed he was extremely ambitious for her, but mixing with people from a completely different walk of life was not in his view a desirable trait, at any rate not in a schoolgirl. As soon as he had realised that Neale was beginning to show a steady interest in Susan, he had intervened and brought her back to earth with some pungent observations on girls who got the reputation of being social climbers. Moreover, on the one occasion he had met Neale, he had thought him a bit supercilious. 'Lacks guts' had been his private judgment.

At all events Susan had listened to him gravely and apparently accepted his strictures, since Neale's name had never been mentioned again, except on one occasion when he asked her directly whether she had seen him again and she had denied it. Since then she had had a succession of boyfriends of seemingly ephemeral interest whose company she sought rather as a status symbol than anything else—or so it seemed to her father. He found he could remember the names of only two of them, one called Ray and another Tony. If they had surnames, he wasn't aware of them.

He noticed as he turned to drive into his garage that every light in the house was now burning. This, however, he knew was no more than his wife's way of fending off the dark forces which she always imagined to be lurking outside when she was alone in the house at night. He found her in the kitchen fully dressed and preparing to iron one of Susan's dresses. She looked up, her face creased in worry. He could see that she had been crying.

'She hasn't come in, I suppose?' he asked in a flat voice.

She shook her head. 'No. Didn't you find her?'

'I hardly expected to find her.' Even at the moment of their shared anxiety her tone was able to provoke him into sarcasm. 'Christine says that Susan left the dance early to come home because she had a headache. She doesn't know what happened to her afterwards.'

'What are we going to do, George?'

'There's only one thing left to do. Inform the police.'

As he spoke, he went out into the hall. Although over two minutes passed before he received any answer from the exchange, he was no longer aware of the passage of time, for his earlier impatience and the urge for immediate action had suddenly given way to a sense of bleak hopelessness. With thoughts far away he idly plucked a leaf off the calendar which hung on the wall above the telephone. It was, after all, a new day, and in a few hours' time life for most people in the village of Offing would resume where it had left off the previous day. But not for George Andrews.

He remembered vaguely noticing that the new day was Saturday, April the thirteenth.

CHAPTER TWO

'Is that you, darling?'

At the sound of his mother's voice, Michael Neale paused on his stealthy journey across the landing. Her bedroom door was partially open and a second later he was caught in a wedge of light as she switched on her bedside lamp.

'Are you there, darling?'

'Yes, Mother.'

'Come in and say good night to me then. I was beginning to think something had happened to you. You didn't say you were going to be so late.'

Standing outside his mother's door poised to enter, he began suddenly to tremble all over. At times he found it insufferable the way she would keep herself awake listening for his return when he had been out. And it was not made any less so by the fact that she always pretended it was pure coincidence that she had happened to hear him at the precise moment he was tip-toeing past her door. And tonight of all nights he had fervently hoped to be allowed to slip unheard into his own room. Bracing himself he entered and went and stood uneasily in the shadows at the foot of the bed. Lady Neale flashed him a look of faint surprise. Normally, he always gave her a filial peck on the cheek and she wondered what was amiss.

She was lying in bed looking as crisp and well-ordered as she invariably managed to do, whether it was giving a dinner party for twenty, or attending an acrimonious committee meeting or just taking the dogs for a walk. Ten years as the wife of a colonial governor together with a born sense of occasion had combined to give her the appearance of being permanently on public duty. She searched her son's face gravely for a second before allowing her own to break into a friendly smile; a smile, too, which revealed a strong sense of proprietary pride.

Michael, who was her only son, had been born when his two sisters were already in their teens. When only a few months old he had contracted a mysterious fever out in Malaya, where his father was serving at the time, and had nearly died. The fact that he had survived not only this but a string of other potentially mortal illnesses while still a child had caused his mother to regard him with extra maternal warmth, and she had never lost her fondness for reminding him and everyone else what a delicate child he had been. During the years that he had been at school in England and while his father was still serving abroad, she had been compelled to surrender her personal direction of his life. But now that Sir James had retired and they were living in the old family home at Offing she was again making every effort to link his life to hers in a hundred different subtle ways.

'Had a nice evening, darling?'

'Yes, quite.' His tone would have belied his words to someone far less perceptive than his mother.

'What were you doing?'

'I've been up in town.'

'With anyone I know?' Lady Neale cocked her head inquiringly against the white pillow.

He shook his head brusquely. 'Some Cambridge people. No one you've met.'

A faint frown flickered across Lady Neale's brow. 'I hope you didn't go anywhere smart, darling, dressed like that! I wouldn't have thought an old rough sports shirt without a tie and that not very elegant suede jacket would be acceptable dress even in the less fashionable parts of town.'

He gave a slight shrug and put his hand up to his forehead.

'Aren't you feeling well?' Lady Neale asked quickly.

'I've got a headache, that's all.'

'Let me get you some Disprin.'

'No, Mother, please don't get out of bed,' he replied with a touch of alarm. The prospect of being fussed over by his mother at this moment was more than he could bear. 'I can get some for myself. I'll be all right in the morning. Anyway, we don't want to wake up Father.'

Sir James Neale and his wife had occupied separate bedrooms for some years, though this was due to nothing more than an amicable disagreement over the matter of nocturnal practices. Sir James was a light sleeper who regarded bed as essentially a place for repose. If you couldn't sleep, then you did the next best thing, which was to lie still with your eyes closed. Lady Neale, on the other hand, could manage on five hours' sleep a night, leaving her approximately three further hours in bed to be accounted for, and it was her custom to put these to use in reading, munching quantites of fruit and, in the early mornings, writing letters. It was the story of Jack Spratt and his wife all over again in a different context.

Oblivious of his mother's careful scrutiny, Michael Neale now suddenly made a dash out of the room and reached the lavatory just in time to be violently sick. For a while his body was seized by uncontrollable shuddering spasms. Then slowly the nausea subsided and eventually he dared to shuffle to his bedroom, only to find his mother standing in the middle of the floor with a glass of some cloudy mixture in her hand.

'I knew you weren't feeling well,' she said briskly. 'Here, drink this.'

It was simpler to do so than to argue. Afterwards, with his mother still hovering, he began to undress, letting his clothes lie where they fell.

'You've most probably caught a chill,' Lady Neale observed, retrieving his shirt and trousers from the floor. 'Either that or a touch of food poisoning. What did you have to eat?'

'I can't remember, but I'll be all right in the morning.'

'If you're not, I'll send for the doctor.'

'That won't be necessary.' And for God's sake, leave me alone, he wanted to scream in her face.

'On second thoughts I think it probably was something you ate. It seemed to come on so suddenly.' He was about to slide into bed, when she went on, 'If I were you, darling, I'd clean your teeth. It'll make you feel a bit fresher, both now and when you wake up.'

She was still in his bedroom when he returned from his reluctant journey to the bathroom. He decided the only thing to do was to ignore her—not that this was difficult in his present condition of mental agony. He got into bed and closed his eyes.

His mother's voice floated down from somewhere above him. 'Don't get up in the morning until I've been in to see how you are. It's Saturday, so there's no hurry.'

He felt her cool hand rest a moment on his forehead, then the door closed with a faint click and she was gone. Immediately, he switched on his bedside lamp—anything to dispel the threatening darkness of his room—and lay back staring blankly at the diffuse circle of light it cast above his head. His body was racked with exhaustion and his mind utterly numb. His thoughts were going round and round in a tight circle from which he felt they would never break out. He wished he could die and leave behind the horror of the last few hours. As it was, he was filled with gnawing dread at the prospect of a new day. Slowly, he turned his head to see the time by the small alarm clock on his bedside table. It showed half-past two.

He tried closing his eyes, but nothing could blot out the nightmare picture in his mind. If anything, it became yet sharper. A name and a face consumed his mind until he thought he must be in a delirium. Finally with an agonised cry, he buried his face in the pillow and his voice was a smothered, choking whisper.

'Susan . . . Susan . . . Oh, my God!'

CHAPTER THREE

Peggy Kingston woke up with a start and with the indefinable feeling of apprehension which she always experienced when she awoke in the still hours of the night. Sometimes it was so powerful that she would have to get up and turn on lights and go downstairs and do something practical in order to re-occupy her mind with mundane matters. She had given up trying to explain to her husband, Bernard, how she felt on these occasions, since he merely looked at her as though she was overdue for an asylum.

As she lay awake trying to focus her mind on what had disturbed her sleep, she heard the baby grandfather clock in the hall strike the half-hour. She turned her head and peered at the twin bed a couple of feet to the left of her own. So Bernard hadn't come in yet! That meant he'd probably be quite drunk when he did reach home. He was never incapable after these nights-out with the boys, but the later he came in, the more time he had had to drink. Always supposing, of course, that this was such an evening. Peggy Kingston sometimes wondered.

Once she had minded very much that he appeared to prefer the company of others to taking her out for an evening, but she now realised somewhat bitterly that she should never have expected anything else after marrying one of nature's hearty extroverts who remained more in tune with the life of his old army mess than with that of his own home. Anyway, she no longer cared how many evenings a month he spent allegedly out with his male cronies, and it had even become something of a relief that his work kept him away from home so much of the time.

As one of Yander's sales representatives, he was not only out the whole of every day, often till eight or nine o'clock in the evening, but on the occasions when he had to relieve a colleague and take on additional travelling, he was away for nights at a time as well. Life was not made easier, as he had reminded her in the days when she used to complain, by the fact that they lived so far from Offing. A good two-hour drive it was with Greater London sprawling in between. And it was she, of course, who had not wanted to move.

She suddenly pricked her ears at a strange sound somewhere in the house. She felt certain, too, that it was the same sound which had woken her up. Yes, there it was again and there was no mistaking it this time. It was water running out of the bathroom basin. One of the girls must be unwell. She quickly got out of bed and slipped on her dressing-gown. No sooner did she open the bedroom door than she saw a light coming from the bathroom. She flew across the landing, not even noticing that her daughters' bedroom door was firmly shut, and flung open the bathroom door.

'Oh, Bernard. It's you! . . . I thought it must be one of the girls . . . Bernard, what have you done to your face?'

'It's only a scratch.'

As he spoke, he began to dab at his chin where the scratch terminated and where there was an encrustation of hard blood.

'How on earth did you do that?'

'A kitten did it,' he replied sourly. He glanced sidelong at her in the mirror. 'I ought to have known better than to try and make friends with it. Vicious little creature it was.'

'Let me do that for you,' his wife said, after watching him dab away without obvious effect.

'Thanks. I'll perch here on the edge of the bath.'

Taken aback by his ready acceptance of her offer to help, seeing that he normally disliked being fussed over unless really ill, she decided that she must also have misjudged him in another respect. Usually when he arrived home in the early hours he was either monosyllabically surly or aggressively truculent. At the present moment he appeared to be neither. She opened the small medicine cupboard and, after casting an eye along a row of jars, bottles and the like, pulled out a tube of antiseptic cream.

'We don't seem to have any Acriflex, I must have used it up when Deirdre grazed her leg last week. But this'll do.'

While her husband sat submissively on the edge of the bath, she set about cleaning the scratch which ran from his right cheek bone all the way down to his chin and which had drawn blood for the whole of its length. She now noticed moreover, that there were two further marks on his right cheek, though these had not bled and were little more than minor abrasions. She completed her handiwork and stood back to examine him.

'I think that's the best I can do. But you'll have to watch out when you shave in the morning. Otherwise you'll start it bleeding again.'

'Better grow a beard.' He ran a finger lightly the length of the scratch and then across the heavy black moustache, which managed to give his face in repose a somewhat sullen expression.

'Wait a moment, you've got some blood on your blazer, too,' his wife said.

'Damn!' Bernard Kingston seized the face-towel she was holding and, wetting one end under the tap, said, 'Whereabouts? Oh, I see it.' He scrubbed away at his lapel for several seconds, then examined himself in the mirror.

'I look a bit of a sight, don't I?' he remarked ruefully. He plucked at a piece of cotton which was sticking to his breast pocket, straightened the club tie he was wearing, passed a comb through his well-greased black hair and, turning to his wife, offered his arm with mock solemnity.

'May I have the pleasure of your company to the bedroom, Mrs. Kingston?'

While he was undressing, his conversation became unwontedly domestic. 'How are the kids?'

'They're all right,' his wife replied, uncertain whether to be more gratified or surprised by his enquiry.

'We'll have to be thinking soon what to do with Sylvia when she leaves school. After all, she'll be fourteen next birthday.'

'Thirteen.'

'Oh! Then Deirdre's eight?'

'Yes, dear. She'll be nine in October.'

She noticed that this recrudescent interest in his family didn't extend to kissing her good night, for he now leapt into bed without so much as glancing in her direction.

'I'll have to be up at six-thirty. I've got to go over to Offing first thing. It's the monthly meeting of sales reps. Bastards, holding it on a Saturday!'

He gave the alarm clock a vigorous wind and shoved it across to her side of the table which lay between the two bed-heads. 'Just four hours of shut-eye and then we're off again on life's jolly old roundabout.'

CHAPTER FOUR

Susan Andrews's body was found around four o'clock on the Saturday afternoon. It was lying in a ditch on the far side of a disused airfield about three and a half miles from Offing. Her scarf had been knotted tightly round her neck and it was obvious even to Will Stocker, the hedge-trimmer, who discovered the body, that she had been killed with great determination. It took Stocker about twenty minutes to reach Offing Police Station on his bicycle, first bumping over the weed-covered runways and then mercifully downhill into the village.

P.C. Newbold, the sole representative of the county constabulary in Offing, lost no time in phoning the information through to divisional headquarters ten miles away, where Detective-Sergeant Hay was sitting alone in the C.I.D. office congratulating himself that he looked like having an undisturbed evening. He listened to Newbold's account with growing gloom.

'I suppose there is a body out there,' he said dubiously. 'I mean, this old fellow of yours isn't given to imagining things?' There was silence the other end of the line as he added, without much hope, 'We don't want to start a false alarm. Wouldn't make us very popular on a Saturday afternoon.'

'If Stocker says there's a body in a ditch, there's a body in a ditch all right, sir. Also it sounds as though it may be Susan Andrews. You remember her father has reported her as missing.'

'I know, but I assumed she'd probably gone off with some young fellow. Hardly blame her wanting to get away from *her* old man. Never fancied it'd be much fun being his daughter. Oh, well, I'd better let headquarters know and then come out to you. Wait for me at the station and your old hedge-cutter fellow can take us to the scene.'

Three-quarters of an hour later, Detective-Sergeant Hay, P.C. Newbold and Will Stocker were standing gazing down at Susan's body.

'It's Susan Andrews all right,' Newbold observed. 'She was a decent girl, too. Some chap should hang for this.'

'Well, he's not likely to,' Sergeant Hay said crisply. 'Not unless he shot her first.' He turned to Stocker. 'Is she in just the same position as when you found her?'

'Aye. Just the same.'

'I wonder what's happened to her shoes. The rest of her clothing doesn't appear to have been disturbed.'

Sergeant Hay let his gaze roam along the

ditch and back along the base of the hedge which bounded it. 'Hey, mind out where you tread,' he called out to Stocker, who had become restless and was moving around as though waiting for a bus on a cold day. 'You may be destroying valuable clues beneath those great crushers of yours.'

The ditch in which Susan's body lay was about two feet deep and largely overgrown with grass and bindweed. It was shielded on one side by a thorn hedge and the ground on the other side rose up in a gentle slope to meet the end of one of the disused runways. The effect was to make her body invisible save when one stood almost over it. She was lying on her back, with her head flopped at an angle and her legs bunched sideways. Her lips were drawn back across her teeth to give her an animal expression.

'Someone certainly meant business, with that scarf,' Newbold said with a catch in his voice. 'Her neck's closed right over it this side.' He was a youngish officer who had three little girls of his own and to whom any offence against children merited slow torture.

Sergeant Hay gave a weary nod. 'Let's hope we get the chap quickly, since the press are certain to go to town over this.' He turned to Newbold, who was standing slowly shaking his head in silent distress. 'You'd better go back to the station and phone headquarters direct. Try and get through to Detective-Superintendent Gordon. He's probably got my message already and will be waiting for further information. I said I was on my way to the scene and would phone as soon as I'd taken stock. Tell him it's Susan Andrews and that she's been murdered. Incidentally, he may be a bit testy. They probably had to pull him out of a football match, but he'll be all right once he knows it's a true bill.'

'Right, Sarge.'

'And take the old boy back with you. No point in his staying here trampling around like a fussed sheep.'

'Right.'

Newbold put his helmet back on, which he had taken off automatically in the presence of death, and climbed up the slope to where he had parked his car on the edge of the runway.

'Headquarters have been on to you several times,' his wife said, pink and flustered as soon as he returned to the functional-looking Victorian villa which was Offing Police Station.

'I'm going to phone them now,' he replied, tossing his helmet on to a chair—it was the only piece of equipment he had never grown used to. 'By the way, I'm afraid it's Susan Andrews.'

'Oh, how awful! Do you think I should go round and see Mrs. Andrews?'

'Not yet. They don't know.'

'What a terrible thing to happen! She was

such a nice girl too.'

He went into his tiny office, but when he got through to headquarters and asked for Detective-Superintendent Gordon it was to be informed that the superintendent was in bed with fibrositis but that the Assistant Chief Constable was waiting to speak to him. Newbold gulped and then rapidly broke into a cold sweat as he realised he couldn't remember the name of the new Assistant Chief. It was a funny name which he always got wrong, anyway. His panic diminished, however, when he recalled that he wouldn't really be required to address him other than as 'sir.' There was a sudden click on the line, a voice saying, 'You're through now, sir,' and another demanding, 'Is that Newbold?'

'P.C. Newbold speaking, sir.'

'This is Mr. Lamartine, the Assistant Chief Constable. What's this about a body being found on Offing Airfield?'

Newbold recited the facts in the stolid polysyllables he had acquired at training school and with the minimum of interruption from the other end of the line.

'Right,' the Assistant Chief said with military precision when he had finished. 'Now then, have you got a tent at your place?'

'A tent, sir?' Newbold was uncertain whether he had heard aright.

'Yes, a tent. Once the body has been

removed to the mortuary you'll need to preserve the scene. The Chief's going to call in the Yard, but we can hardly expect anyone to get down from London much before seven or eight. Meanwhile Detective-Inspector Donald will be coming over to take charge. Also Sergeant Eagle from the Photographic Section. Have you got all that?'

'Yes, sir.'

'Well, you'd better go and join Sergeant Hay at the scene. Oh, yes, one other thing: Doctor Ryman, the pathologist, will be on his way shortly, or he will be as soon as anyone can semaphore him a message down amongst his beastly bee-hives.' He let out an exasperated snort. 'I don't know! Bodies as your living, bees as your hobby! Right, any questions?'

Newbold, who had been listening with a fixed, worried expression for fear the Assistant Chief would ring off without giving him an opportunity of asking the one question which was possessing his mind, said in a breathless voice: 'What about the girl's parents, sir?'

'What about them?'

'They don't yet know anything.'

'Oh, I see!' There was a slight pause. 'Well, you had better go and break it to them. You'll want the father to identify the body. Anything else?'

'No, sir.'

The line went immediately dead, leaving

Newbold brooding over the distasteful duty which lay ahead of him. In a grim tone, he called out to his wife: 'I'm going round to break it to the Andrewses now, Joyce.'

P.C. Newbold had the length of the village street to negotiate in order to reach the Andrewses' house. As he drove along it, he could not help but be aware of the extra interest his progress was arousing. News of Susan's disappearance was now common coin, and he had small doubt that speculation as to what had happened to her was rife in the village. There were only half a dozen shops, but in each on this late Saturday afternoon there was, he felt certain, a single topic of conversation. Mr. Straker, the butcher, gave him a wave as he passed which he answered in kind. A little farther on, it was Mr. Gaunter, the local cobbler, who raised a thumb in friendly greeting.

Newbold liked the village and liked, too, most of the people who lived in it, though he suffered from no starry-eyed illusions about them. There were the good and there were the bad, just a few of them, like Bob Thrupp, but the thing a policeman had to remember was that the good weren't necessarily all they might seem to be if you had occasion to peer under the lid. Newbold was strongly of the opinion that the doctor, the parson and the policeman should between them know just about as much as was possible of what went on beneath the surface of village life. Once upon a time the village schoolmaster would also have been included, but with new schools looking like expensive greenhouses and staff and pupils gravitating from miles around it was no longer so.

He braked hard and frowned as a 3-litre Rover pulled out from the kerb without any warning and accelerated away from him. One day, he reflected grimly, Lady Neale would be having the pleasure of appearing as a defendant in her own court, where once a fortnight she sat in minor judgment on others. P.C. Newbold did not care for Lady Neale. She was an atrocious snob and inclined to treat him as if he might be one of her loyal personal servants. Sir James, on the other hand, was a decent old buffer and quite without any side. As for their son, Michael, he seemed an agreeable enough young man, anxious to be friendly but uncertain how to set about it. It always seemed to Newbold that he wore a perennially wistful air.

A little farther on he was surprised to notice more cars than usual parked outside the Blue Boar. Then he recalled that there had been a reps' meeting at Yander's. It must have gone on into the afternoon, and now it was 'one for the road' before they departed for an abbreviated week-end at home.

He reached the end of the village, and in a

quarter of a mile turned left down the lane which led to three isolated cottages of which the Andrewses occupied the most distant. He was relieved to notice George Andrews bending over a bed in the garden, as this meant he wouldn't be confronted by Mrs. Andrews, which was something he had been quietly dreading. He parked the car and got out.

George Andrews was now staring at him with hands resting on a garden fork, staring with the expression of a condemned man awaiting his executioner. Newbold licked his lips and marched up the path to where Andrews stood motionless.

'I'm afraid I have bad news for you, Mr. Andrews. We've found Susan's body. It was in a ditch the other side of the old airfield.'

For several seconds Andrews said nothing, but just stared into the other's face. Then slowly his gaze dropped to his hands on the fork. 'How was she killed?' he asked quietly.

'She was—she was strangled with her own scarf.' Newbold paused uncomfortably. 'I'm very sorry that this has happened to you, Mr. Andrews.'

'Thanks. I never really expected to see her again. I only kept up the pretence for my wife's sake.' He looked Newbold straight in the face. 'To you and me, the pattern was too familiar, eh?'

'We'd like you to come out to the scene as

soon as convenient,' Newbold said diffidently.

'I'll come now. I'll just leave a note for my wife. She's in the village. There's no chance of her learning the news while she's out, is there?'

Newbold shook his head firmly. 'Only people who know are my wife and Will Stocker who found the—who found Susan, and I've sent him home and told him to keep quiet about it. He will, too. He's a taciturn old man, he won't say a word to anyone.'

'That's all right, then. But I wouldn't want Winnie to hear of Susan's death as an item of village gossip. Well, I'm ready when you are.'

Although it would add ten minutes to their journey, Newbold decided to avoid driving back through the village and to go via the back lanes.

'That was thoughtful of you,' Andrews said gruffly as they approached their destination.

'Seemed wiser. Don't want to add to the village rumours.'

'Rumours? About my daughter, do you mean?' His tone was sharp and Newbold flushed as though a personal accusation had been made against him.

'No-o, I just meant rumours in general. Every village is always full of them. I wasn't referring to your daughter at all.'

'Oh, I see. I'm afraid I'm not very well up with Offing rumours. Probably because I don't listen carefully enough.'

An uncomfortable silence fell between the two men as Newbold turned the car off the road and began to bump across the broken surface of the runway, avoiding as far as he could the deeper potholes and the feet-high tufts of weeds. He was aware that Andrews had not been a popular member of the force, and though he had never served directly under him, he had not been too happy when he found him suddenly living in the village as a retired detective-inspector. But he was the first now to admit that Andrews had occasioned him no worry at all. He had never claimed any position of privilege and had behaved with scrupulous propriety in their official dealings on points of security affecting the factory. Newbold had been agreeably surprised—and grateful.

He parked the car and led the way down the slope toward the ditch. There was no sign at first of Sergeant Hay, but he suddenly appeared from behind the hedge about a hundred yards farther along. He came up and greeted Andrews warily.

'Yes, that's Susan,' Andrews said, staring fiercely at his daughter's body. He started to move forward.

'Don't go any nearer, please,' Sergeant Hay said. 'Don't want to touch anything until Doctor Ryman's looked it over.'

Andrews halted, frowning his displeasure. 'Where are her shoes?' he asked.

'Can't find them anywhere,' Sergeant Hay replied. 'I've been searching the whole area.'

'Looks like a button's been torn from her blouse.'

Sergeant Hay nodded. 'Yep, I noticed that, too. Though the rest of her clothing doesn't look as if it's been interfered with. We'll soon know.'

Andrews threw him an angry glance and Newbold blushed for his sergeant's insensitivity. Fancy speaking to the dead girl's father as though his daughter was only an interesting specimen awaiting the attentions of pathologist, forensic scientist, photographer and a whole queue of other experts. But Sergeant Hay now walked a few paces away and nodded to Newbold to follow him.

'Well, what exactly's happening? Did you get through to Detective-Superintendent Gordon?'

Briefly Newbold told him the result of his telephone call to headquarters.

'So the Chief's decided to call in the Yard!' Sergeant Hay sounded surprised. 'Probably quite an astute move, though. It'll prevent trouble with Andrews if things don't work out. At least, not so much prevent it as divert it elsewhere. We shan't have to bear the brunt of his complaints, it'll be the Yard boys.'

'I got the impression he'd called in the Yard simply because Superintendent Gordon was ill.'

'Providential, shall we say?' Sergeant Hay

remarked with a smirk.

Newbold said stoutly, 'Well, I've never had any trouble with Andrews and . . .'

'Look, you've never served under him, have you! Take it from me, he was a pig. Sometimes on purpose, sometimes because he couldn't help himself. If you ask me, he was jolly lucky to get that job at Yander's. I only hope I'm as fortunate when I come to retire. Bet I shan't be, though.' He cocked his head. 'Think I hear a car coming.'

A minute later Detective-Inspector Donald and Doctor Ryman appeared over the skyline.

Doctor Ryman was a tall, thin man with bushy grey hair and a moustache. He never wore a hat and seldom a topcoat apart from a greasy old mackintosh if it was raining really hard. He resembled a bee-keeper much more than an eminent pathologist. Half-way down the slope he paused and with great care put on a pair of spectacles. Then, moving gingerly forward to within a yard of the body, he peered about him as though looking for something he had dropped.

'Had a herd of elephants around here?' he called out, pointing to where the grass was flattened at the edge of the ditch.

'Those are my prints over there, sir,' Sergeant Hay replied, indicating another flattened portion of grass. 'The ones you're looking at were here when we arrived. They must have been made by the murderer.' With a faint note of triumph, he added, 'You'll see, sir, that I've staked them round.'

Doctor Ryman grinned toothily over his shoulder. 'Good boy!' Then resuming his scrutiny of the ground, he muttered, 'Eyes, eyes. They're the best detectives.'

'Just like being at one of his bloody lectures,' Sergeant Hay whispered to Newbold.

'Right, let's have a look at the lass herself,' the pathologist said, springing lightly into the ditch by her head.

For a full minute he stared down at the body, occasionally pursing his lips and frowning, but all the time staring, staring. Eventually he went down on his haunches and gently turned her head.

'Tch-tch! Poor lass.' Then, looking up at the circle of men watching him, he asked, 'Anyone seen the lass's shoes?'

'No, sir.'

'Well, there's one line of inquiry for you to start on.'

He leaned forward over the body and lifted up the red skirt. Then, looking across at George Andrews, he called out, 'Her underclothing appears to be intact, Mr. Andrews. You'll probably be glad to know that.'

Andrews received the information with a set expression, and the pathologist turned his attention to Susan's hands. 'I think I'll take fingernail scrapings here. Don't want to risk losing anything when she's moved. Somebody go and get my bag out of the car.'

Eventually, he was satisfied that the first stage of his work was done and stepped from the ditch. 'As far as I'm concerned, you can take her off to the mortuary as soon as you like. Have you taken any photographs yet?'

'The photographer's just arriving now, sir,' Inspector Donald replied.

'Good. As soon as he's finished you can move the lass.'

'I was thinking, sir, perhaps we ought to leave her until the Yard officers have arrived. Another hour or so isn't going to make much difference.'

'It isn't going to help anyone either,' Doctor Ryman retorted. 'They'll not be able to achieve anything I can't tell them. And it'll be dark by then anyway. Much better move her while it's light.' He observed Inspector Donald's worried expression. 'You put them on to me as soon as they come. I'll tell them all they want to know. It'll not help them to see the lass lying there in the ditch. They'll understand. They've got some sense, those Scotland Yard chaps. Most of them, anyway,' he added with a chuckle.

'Very well, sir. As soon as the photographer has finished, I'll have the body moved.'

'Good boy!' With an airy wave of his hand Doctor Ryman strode up the bank, paused at the top and came back to where Andrews was standing slightly apart from the others.

'You and I have brought several cases to satisfactory conclusions in the past. Don't fear, we'll do it again.' He put a hand on the other's arm and gave it a quick squeeze of encouragement. 'Tell Mrs. Andrews how sorry I am.'

A quarter of an hour after he had gone the ambulance arrived and Susan's body was taken away. Finally the three police officers were left to erect the tent over the ditch where she had lain, though only after every inch of area had first been scoured for clues. But nothing was found of any evidential significance and it was with a feeling of general despondency that they set about putting up the tent. They had just completed the task when a car pulled up at the top of the slope and two men got out, silhouetted against the pink-and-grey-streaked evening sky.

'I'm Detective-Superintendent Manton,' the taller man announced. 'And this is Detective-Sergeant Avis. We were told we'd find you out here.' His tone became lightly sardonic. 'Don't think I'm grumbling but Saturday evening is the hell of a time to begin a murder hunt.'

CHAPTER FIVE

Offing Police Station had never before had so many officers within its walls as when the party arrived back from the airfield. P.C. Newbold began to fetch extra chairs, but then realised there was going to be no room to put them if he did muster sufficient.

'I shouldn't bother,' Manton said pleasantly. 'It's not as though we're about to get the cards out. Sergeant Avis can perch up on the counter.'

Detective-Sergeant Avis, a small, olive-complexioned man with a neat moustache and a pair of enormously alert eyes, immediately obliged by nimbly hoisting himself on to the counter which formed P.C. Newbold's receipt of custom.

At Manton's request, each of the officers present recited what he knew of the affair. When they had finished, he said, 'So she disappeared around half-past eleven last night and her body wasn't found until four o'clock this afternoon. Seems reasonable to suppose that she was murdered within an hour or so of her disappearance and her body then dumped in that ditch. It also seems a reasonable guess that she was murdered somewhere between the village and the spot where her body was found.'

He looked at his watch. 'Mmm. Half-past seven. I'd like to see Andrews first, he's the obvious starting point of the inquiry, and then we'll pay a call on the Thrupps, seeing that their daughter is the last known person to have seen Susan Andrews alive. Shall we go, Dick?'

★   ★   ★

'I think that's about all for the moment, Mr. Andrews,' Manton said. He reached out for Sergeant Avis's notebook and squinted at the entries which had been made. 'We've got a note of Michael Neale's name and I've no doubt that Christine Thrupp will be able to fill us in with the names of other boys your daughter knew.' He gave Andrews a small, deprecating smile. 'No need to tell *you* that it's a slow process of elimination in cases of this sort. We're already having a check made on all the known sex offenders in the district. As you know, they're the hardest to track down and they remain a menace so long as they're at large.'

Andrews, who had been staring at the floor, looked up sharply. 'I'm not interested in what else the fellow may do. I want him caught because he murdered my daughter, and for no other reason. If I sound vindictive, it's because I am.'

'That's understandable,' Manton remarked quietly, while Sergeant Avis gazed at Andrews with a quizzical expression.

As they made their way to the front door, Manton caught a glimpse of a white-faced woman moving about the kitchen as though in a trance. Police officers lived with personal tragedy and were supposed to grow callous and unconcerned with the human side of their work, but Manton never failed to be affected when he had dealings with the close relations of a victim, nor, for that matter, to draw strength in his determination to run his quarry to earth. And where a child was involved, his determination was that much the greater.

'Poor sod!' Sergeant Avis remarked as they drove away. 'To think my daughter will be sixteen in a few years' time. I know just how he must be feeling.'

When they arrived at the Thrupps' the front door was opened by a small boy of about ten, whose face clouded over with doubt when Manton asked if he might speak to his father.

'I don't know,' he said. 'He's watching the telly. Can't you come back?'

'No.'

The boy made a face to indicate the problem wasn't rightly his anyway and shouted over his shoulder, 'Two men to see you here, Dad.'

A minute later Thrupp appeared from a room at the back and Manton introduced himself. 'We'd like to have a word with your daughter Christine, Mr. Thrupp. Is she at home?'

'What do you want to see her for?'

'She was the last person to see Susan Andrews.'

'What of it? She's already told all she knows. I'm not going to have my daughter drawn into this.'

'But for the grace of God it might have been your daughter who was found strangled in a ditch.'

Thrupp looked disbelieving. 'My Gawd! You don't mean the Andrews girl's dead?'

Manton nodded. 'And your daughter was with her shortly before she disappeared, I understand.'

'She doesn't know anything more than she's told,' Thrupp repeated with an air of obstinacy. 'It's not right to drag a young girl into unpleasantness.'

While this dialogue had been taking place the small boy had been watching his father and Manton as though they were contestants across a tennis net. He now caught Sergeant Avis's eye and gave him a cocky grin. Sergeant Avis replied with a look of calculating appraisal which he was glad to note caused the boy to shift uncomfortably.

'I get the impression, Mr. Thrupp,' Manton said levelly, 'that you don't wish Susan Andrews's murderer to be found. That strikes me as being a pretty curious attitude for the father of her best friend to take.'

'You don't need to try that line on me. I just don't believe in getting caught up in other people's business. Nothing's going to bring Susan back to life, so what's the point?' He paused and a mean look flickered across his face. 'Anyway the police have never done much to help me, why should they expect my family to help them?'

Manton's expression hardened. 'Look, Mr. Thrupp, we've spent long enough bandying words. I want to see your daughter. Is she in?'

Thrupp hesitated, then said sullenly to his son, 'Go and fetch Christine.'

'What's more, I'm not going to talk to her on the doorstep,' Manton went on. 'If we can't come in, I'll have to ask her to go back to the police station with us.'

'You're not taking my daughter to any police station.'

'O.K. Can we go into your front room here?' Manton gestured towards a window through which could be seen the cold comfort of a 'best' room.

Thrupp shrugged. 'I suppose so.'

The thing that Manton noticed about Christine when she joined them a minute or so later was that she was trembling violently and he assumed that her brother had broken the news of Susan's death.

'I'm sure, Christine, you want to help us find the man who killed Susan—' he said sympathetically.

Her hand flew up to her mouth and the trembling became more violent. Her father, who was standing in the doorway, watched her helplessly, and it was left to Manton to guide her into a chair. She was dressed in a pair of tight tartan trousers and a thick canary yellow sweater. Her hair, which fell about her shoulders, looked as though it could do with a wash. Manton tried to picture her in a neat school uniform and failed.

'You and Susan went to a dance at the school last night—that's right, isn't it?' he asked gently when she had gained control over her emotions. 'I want you to tell me everything you can remember about it. What Susan said, whom she talked to, whom she danced with, everything. You understand?'

The girl was looking at him with red-eyed horror, but seemed unable to speak. Her lips were parted but nothing came.

'Well, let's start at the beginning,' Manton said, in a coaxing tone. 'What time did you go to the dance?' But the question brought forth only another burst of sobs and the two officers looked at one another with resignation.

'She's not fit to be asked questions,' Thrupp broke in resentfully. 'Anyone can see that. She's just heard that her friend's dead; it's enough to knock any young girl for six!'

'I realise that, and it's why I'm giving her a

chance to get over her distress,' Manton said, 'but she'll be all right in a minute or two.' He looked toward Christine who was sniffing into her handkerchief. 'Now then, will you try and answer my questions. What time did you and Susan get to the dance?'

There was half a minute's silence before she made any reply. Then, staring hard at the floor between her feet, she mumbled, 'Susan never went to the dance. I don't know where she went.'

CHAPTER SIX

In the silence which followed this disclosure Manton did some quick thinking. It was now clear why she had been so evasive when Andrews had called in the early hours of the morning, and it also explained her present distress which from the very beginning had seemed to him to spring in part from some element of personal culpability. So she had been covering up for her friend in what had begun as a schoolgirl secret and turned into a runaway nightmare.

'Do you mean that you never saw Susan at all last night?' Manton asked at length.

'No. I didn't.'

'But you agreed to back up her story that she

was going to the dance with you?'

'She said that was what she was going to tell her parents.'

'And she asked you to support her?'

'Yes.'

'Well, where did Susan go?'

Christine shook her head. 'I don't know. I promise you I don't know.'

'But she must have told you what she was going to do instead of the dance?'

'She just said she was going out with someone.'

'Did she mention his name?'

'No.'

'Did she give you any idea who it was?'

'She did say I'd never met him.'

'Did you ask her who it was?'

'Yes, but she just said I wouldn't know him . . . I . . .'

'Yes?'

'From what she told me, I gathered he'd invited her out. It was something special. A dinner-dance, she said.'

'And she didn't want her parents to know?'

'She said her father would be mad if he knew. He'd never let her go.'

'Why did you agree to cover up for her, Christine?'

Christine looked at him with surprise. 'But I often have,' she replied boldly.

'When Susan was going out with boys, do

you mean?'

'Yes. Her parents were very strict with her, so she always used to tell them that she was going out with me.'

'Can you tell me the names of any of the boys she went out with without her parents knowing?'

'Mostly it was with Michael Neale.'

'Has she been seeing him recently?'

'Oh, yes.'

'So it might have been him she went out with last night?'

'No, it wasn't Michael last night.'

'Why do you say that?'

'She was kind of mysterious about last night. She wouldn't tell me who it was. But she promised she would later.' Her chin suddenly began to quiver and she put her handkerchief up to her mouth. 'She said it would spoil it to let me into the secret beforehand and that anyway *he* had made her swear not to tell anyone that she was going out with him.'

'It sounds as though he mayn't have been local.'

'I don't know.'

'You say, Christine, that she was mysterious about whom she was going out with. Was she usually that way?'

'Oh, no. She always used to tell me.'

'Did she appear to be looking forward to her date last night?'

'Yes, she was all excited over it. She said it was the first time she'd received an invitation like it.'

'Mmm. Have you heard her mention the names of any boys she knew outside Offing?'

'There was someone called Martin Butcher who once asked her to a party in London, but her parents wouldn't let her go and I don't think she was very keen anyway.'

'Possibly not, if she asked her parents first,' Manton remarked drily. 'Tell me, was she very fond of Michael Neale?'

'He was crazy about her.'

'But what were her feelings toward him?'

'She liked him.' Her tone became disdainful, as though reflecting Susan's own feeling. 'But he was . . .' She gave a petulant shrug. 'Well, he was so soppy.'

'Meaning what?'

'Soppy! Soft! Susan didn't think he could ever have been with another girl before he met her.'

'Did *you* know him?' Manton asked, faintly repelled by the change which had come over Christine since the interview had begun. It was as though she had suddenly realised the strength of her rôle as best friend and confidante.

'Not properly. Susan used to keep him to herself.'

'Despite the fact she found him soft?'

'She liked him all right. I said so. And he was never exactly short of cash.'

'Oh, I see.'

'Not that she went out with him just because he had money,' she said indignantly.

'She wouldn't have been the first girl to have done that.'

'Anyway, she didn't.'

'Did his parents know that he was taking Susan out?'

''Course they didn't. They wouldn't have approved any more as would Susan's.'

Manton got up from his chair. 'And you're certain it wasn't Neale she went out with last night?'

Christine pouted out her lower lip and frowned.

'Not unless Susan was having me on. Mind you, she did sometimes. Even if she was my friend, she didn't always tell me everything, not the way some girls do.'

As Manton and Avis prepared to leave, Thrupp broke in and said, 'Well, I hope you've found out all you want as I don't wish Christine to be bothered again. If some poor bastard is going to get nailed, don't ask any of my family to pass you the hammer. We don't like getting mixed up in other people's troubles.'

Manton looked at him, his bright blue eyes suddenly cold and uncompromising. 'Believe me, I'd far sooner conduct this inquiry without your help too. But if I do happen to think I need it, I'll be back. Good evening.'

As they regained their car, his expression changed and he gave Sergeant Avis a cheerful grin.

'What's funny, sir?'

'Nothing for you. You have a daughter coming up to sixteen. I only have a son.'

Sergeant Avis cocked him a beady eye. 'Then I hope you'll make sure, sir, he doesn't turn out to be soft and soppy.'

After this, they drove in silence for some distance.

CHAPTER SEVEN

'Nice place,' Manton observed, when twenty minutes later they stood on the steps of Offing Hall. It was a Georgian house of medium size with a carefuly tended magnolia covering the wall on one side of the front door and a surround of flower-beds which were tidy without looking as though they belonged to a seed merchant's catalogue.

They had parked their car beside an open M.G. sports which was standing in a bay of the gravel drive in front of the house.

'Presumably Master Michael's car,' Manton said with a nod.

At this moment the front door opened and a girl in a white overall, wearing her hair in a precarious mound on top of her head, looked out at them.

'Please?' she said in a clearly foreign accent.

'Is Mr. Neale at home?' Manton asked.

'Sir James Neale, yes?'

'No, Mr. Michael Neale.'

'Oh! Please wait while I see.'

Leaving them standing on the doorstep, she disappeared to be replaced a minute later by a small, elegant woman. 'I'm Lady Neale. Can I help you?'

'We'd like to see your son, Madam. Is he in?'

'Yes, but he's not very well today, he's resting.' She looked from Manton to Avis and back again. 'I don't think you've told me what your business is.'

'Is it impossible to see Mr. Neale then?' Manton asked, ignoring her hint.

There was a note of asperity in her tone when she replied. 'I don't wish to disturb him unless it's absolutely necessary. Perhaps you could call back some other time.' With a certain iciness she added, 'Or better still telephone to find out when it would be convenient.'

Manton chewed his lower lip thoughtfully. He could see that it would not be difficult to make an enemy out of Lady Neale, and this, on the whole, he would prefer to avoid. It was never good policy to antagonise anyone unnecessarily, though sometimes with a man like Thrupp one was forced to discard the velvet glove, not to reveal any mailed fist, but simply to show there was a hand inside.

'As a matter of fact, it is rather important, Madam. It's a police matter,' he said, breaking the silence which had begun to become noticeable.

'A police matter,' Lady Neale repeated as though the words had a disagreeable flavour. 'Has he been getting into trouble with that car of his?'

'No, it has nothing to do with his car.' He paused, then with a slight shrug went on, 'We're inquiring into the death of someone whom we understand he knew.'

Lady Neale stared at Manton with an expression of well-bred incomprehension. 'You're being very mysterious, Mr. er . . . er . . .'

'Detective-Superintendent Manton.'

'Er . . . Superintendent. May one ask who this person is . . . this person who has died?'

'I think I should see your son first, Madam. He will doubtless tell you all you wish to know afterwards.'

As he spoke he could not help hoping that he wasn't going to be met by obstructive parents on every doorstep, otherwise he would have to devise a few fresh techniques. He now went on, 'Your son, I believe, is twenty-two. So I think he's entitled to be treated as an adult.'

'Very well. But I must ask you to remember that he's not feeling very fit today; moreover, that he's home only for the week-end and has to go back to Cambridge tomorrow evening. He's working hard for the first part of his Tripos and I don't want him upset. I'm sure you understand.' She turned into the hall. 'If you wait in the study here, I'll go and fetch him.'

'Wouldn't fancy being one of her cubs,' Sergeant Avis remarked as he and Manton took stock of the room in which Lady Neale had left them.

A flat-topped leather inlaid desk was its chief feature. On the desk was a silver-framed photograph of a man, presumably Sir James Neale, in plumed helmet and white uniform greeting King George VI as he stepped out of an aeroplane. Beside him was Lady Neale in an enormous picture hat in the act of dropping a curtsy. Another even larger photograph showed Sir James, again in full regalia, and attended by a whole retinue of officers in uniform, apparently addressing some African assembly. Everyone in it looked full of starch and discomfort.

On the wall at the side of the desk was a rack of well-chewed pipes. Two large leather armchairs and a floor-to-ceiling bookcase made up the rest of the furniture. Manton walked across to the bookcase. You could often learn more about someone from the books they read and kept than in several hours of conversation with them. Not, however, that Sir James Neale's choice of reading matter was likely to tell them much about his son. Manton hadn't cast his eye along the first row before the door opened and Michael Neale came in. Manton saw a shortish young man with dark hair, and a pale face against which a growth of stubble was etched across the upper lip and at the sides of the chin. He had rings under his eyes which, as Manton was later to notice, were permanently glazed as though Neale was always in a state of chronic weariness.

'I'm Michael Neale,' he said, in a tired voice.

'What were you doing last night, Mr. Neale?' Manton asked abruptly.

'I . . . er . . . I was in London with some friends.'

'You could tell me who they were, if necessary?'

Neale passed the tip of his tongue over his lips. 'Why do you want to know?'

'What time did you get home?'

'I can't remember. Late.'

'After midnight?'

'Yes.'

Manton nodded as though satisfied with the answers so far. 'You knew Susan Andrews, didn't you?'

A mesmerised nod.

'Did you by any chance see her last night?'

'No.' It came as a whisper.

'When did you last see her?'

'In the Easter vac.'

'Did your parents approve of you going out with her?'

Neale gazed slowly about the room as though seeing it for the first time. Finally his gaze came back to Manton.

'No.' Again no more than a whisper.

'Did they know you were seeing her during your last vacation?'

'I don't think so.'

'Were you very fond of her?'

Neale sucked in his lower lip and bit it hard, at the same time giving a faint nod of his head.

'And she of you?'

'We . . . were in love,' he murmured, and his eyes filled with tears which he tried to blink away, turning his head from the two police officers.

'Why should that make you cry?' Manton asked, quickly.

Neale closed his eyes and sighed with the air of one who felt his martyrdom would never end.

'Because everything's against us at the moment.'

'Hmm.' Manton's tone was not sympathetic. 'Have you been out at all today?'

'No.' There was a pause and Neale met

Manton's gaze with a suffering expression.

'I somehow believe,' Manton said with quiet emphasis, 'that you know Susan's dead, don't you?'

Neale looked at him in stupefaction. 'No, no, I don't believe it.' He looked up, his eyes abrim once more with tears. 'Dead? What do you mean? How can she be dead?'

'She was murdered last night.'

Neale sank on to the arm of one of the leather chairs and covered his face with his hands.

'I can't believe it,' he gasped. 'Who—who would have wanted to kill Susan?'

'That's something I'm sure you'll do your best to help us find out,' Manton replied briskly. 'Do you know the names of any boys she was going out with?'

'No.' His tone was blankly forlorn.

'Have you any ideas to offer on the question of who might have murdered her?'

'No. She didn't have any male friends apart from myself.'

'Did you ever take Susan to a dinner-dance at any time?'

'Yes, several times.'

'Where?'

'The Green Spiral outside Amersham and the Water Mill near Hemel Hempstead. I think they're the only two.'

'Both some distance from here?'

'Yes. We had to . . .'

'I understand,' Manton broke in. 'Did you ever take her up to London?'

'Yes.'

'To shows and the like?'

'Yes.'

Manton looked across at Sergeant Avis and raised an eyebrow, to ascertain whether he had any questions of his own to ask. Avis shook his head.

'I take it, Mr. Neale,' Manton now went on, 'that if we wish to see you again, you'd prefer us not to beard you up at Cambridge.'

Neale nodded. 'It might be embarrassing,' he said, with a wisp of a smile.

'Well, we'll meet that problem when it arises. I expect we can manage something. By the way, have you got a snapshot of yourself you could let us have? Purely a matter of routine.'

Looking slightly apprehensive, Neale fished in his wallet and produced a photograph which he handed across to Manton.

'Is this Susan Andrews with you?'

'Yes. May I have it back when you've finished with it?'

'Certainly.'

They took their leave of Neale at the front door. While Avis was turning their car, Manton walked across to the M.G. and peered into it. It was a 1950 model and the floor was a mess of oily, worn-out matting and bits of debris. Just the sort of car his son aspired to own when he was old enough to hold a licence. Twenty-five years earlier he wouldn't have minded it himself, but at forty-seven the lure of zipping along suspended only a few inches above the road and with the wind tearing at your features had faded.

'You don't think he did it, do you, sir?' Sergeant Avis asked when Manton joined him.

'Not if we go by what Christine Thrupp says. But I suppose he could have done; his demeanour wasn't all that convincing. On the other hand, if he genuinely wasn't feeling well, it might have been due to that.' Manton made a sudden small gesture of annoyance. 'I meant to have asked him what brought him home this week-end. Blast!'

'Where now, sir?' Sergeant Avis asked impassively.

'I think we might go and find Doctor Ryman and see what he can tell us. He should have completed the p.m. by now.'

'Eyes, eyes, they're the best detectives,' Sergeant Avis mimicked, then added forcefully, 'One day somebody'll find him dead and it won't be from bee stings.'

'You don't like him?' Manton asked with an amused smile.

'No. He goes in for favourites and I don't happen to be one of them.'

'I hadn't noticed that.'

'You wouldn't have, sir. You're obviously

well in.'

In the silence which followed, Manton fell to wondering how he was going to get on with his sergeant. It was the first time they had worked together, Avis having only recently been transferred from a Division to C.I. at the Yard. He had a reputation for hard work accompanied by a certain moodiness, also for forming strong likes and dislikes which were subsequently found difficult to dislodge. He was intensely proud of his Greek ancestry, and appeared to regret that each generation had lopped a bit off the original family name to anglicise it. Avis was all that was now left. On the whole, however, Manton liked his straightforwardness and his lack of deference, and had no serious qualms about him as a team-mate. But he'd have to keep an eye open to see that he didn't get across the local boys.

He took off his hat, laid it on his lap, and suddenly caught sight of his reflection in the side window. Not bad for forty-seven. Firm, brown skin with no sign of pouchiness, nor yet of any scragginess round the neck. Hair going a bit thin in front but without a single fleck of grey. And as for figure, well, only two months ago he had squeezed through a twelve-inch gap to win a bet. The fact that he had ricked a shoulder muscle in so doing was unknown to all save himself, though it had successfully knocked him out of an early round in one of the police golf competitions, which he normally won.

Sergeant Avis brought the car to a halt in front of a building which resembled a secularised chapel. 'This is the mortuary, sir. It's at the back of the Coroner's Court.'

Manton got out and squared his shoulders. He disliked mortuaries, and had never acquired the veneer of casual ghoulishness which most police officers assume at an early stage in their careers. Detective-Sergeant Avis, he was interested to note, appeared to be equally unattracted by the prospect ahead.

Together they made their reluctant way down a dark, smelly passage and into the ill-lit Dickensian cavern which served as public mortuary for Offing and the surrounding district.

CHAPTER EIGHT

'It's not so much a public mortuary as a public scandal,' Dr. Ryman was expostulating to Detective-Sergeant Hay when Manton and Avis walked in. 'Why don't you get something done about it?'

'You'd better have a word with the Chief Constable, sir,' Hay replied indifferently.

'Have you ever seen such a hell-hole?' he

demanded, swinging round to the new arrivals.
'I don't mind telling you, I won't do another
p.m. here. You can pass that on to the Chief
Constable.'

'I expect it's difficult getting money to build
new mortuaries,' Manton remarked. 'They
don't rate very high on the list of priorities.
People are more interested in schools and
hospitals.'

'Pah! People don't know.'

Manton's gaze took in the old-fashioned
mortuary table, the two naked electric light
bulbs suspended from the grimy, flat, glass
roof, and the heavy porcelain sink—more like a
small horse trough—which stuck out from the
wall and into which water from a single garden
tap was dribbling. Finally, it came back to the
pathologist who was impatiently struggling out
of his white gown.

'Well, Dr. Ryman?'

'Yes, Superintendent, what would you like to
know?'

'Everything.'

'Sensible fellow. Too many of you just want
to plug me with questions. Usually the wrong
ones at that. Lawuyers are the worst. Think
they know my job better than I do. Result is
they defeat their own ends. It's no thanks to
them that justice usually comes out right side
up.

'Now then, first things first. The lass died

from asphyxia due to strangulation by a ligature. The ligature had been knotted so tightly that it had bitten into the soft tissues of the neck and completely constricted the breathing passages. Unconsciousness and death had supervened in a matter of seconds.'

He paused, as though to trap Manton into asking a question. When none came, he went on with a satisfied glint in his eye, 'There were no injuries apart from those connected with the asphyxia. Moreover the lass was fully dressed save for a button missing from her blouse, which I deduce had been ripped off, and for her shoes, which you know about. However, I found no sign that she had walked any distance in her stockinged feet. Both stockings were quite clean and undamaged.'

In a thoughtful tone, Manton said, 'Then her shoes must have been removed after her body had been deposited in the ditch.'

'Or her body was carried to the ditch minus her shoes,' Sergeant Avis chimed in.

'Exactly,' Dr. Ryman said, apparently gratified by such obvious deduction. 'Incidentally, Superintendent, her clothing is all bundled up ready for you to take to the laboratory, together with the usual specimens.'

He now fixed them with the eye of the conjurer coming in to his better tricks. 'There was no evidence of any sexual interference, though the hymen had been partially torn at some time in the past.'

'Meaning she wasn't a virgin?' Manton asked keenly.

Dr. Ryman frowned. 'That is *one* interpretation, but not the only one. The lass doesn't deserve to lose her character on such inconclusive evidence. If there had been some attempt at intercourse in the past, it's certain that full penetration had never been achieved.'

'Can you say how long ago the hymen had been damaged?' Manton asked.

'No. There'd been a tear, and it had completely healed. Might have been several weeks, even months ago. No use your pressing me about that, because I can't tell you any more. But let me give you two other items of information which I think you'll find of more immediate interest. First, the lass had had a meal within two or three hours of death which had consisted of a mixed grill with chipped potatoes. She had also drunk some wine.'

'That gives us a line of inquiry,' Manton observed.

'Exactly! And here's another lead for you. Caught between her two front upper teeth was a small piece of cotton. White cotton.' He noticed Manton's questioning expression. 'It's no good looking at me like that, but the laboratory should be able to tell you more about it in due course.'

'At least you can tell me how long a piece,'

Manton urged.

'Not more than a quarter of an inch.' He dived across to a chair on which lay a small, battered attaché case and seizing it said abruptly, 'And that's all. I'll let you have a preliminary report tomorrow and a full one within the week. It'll depend on what sort of mood my secretary's in.' He shot Manton a sardonic glance. 'You know Miss Swingler!'

Manton grinned while Sergeant Avis muttered under his breath, 'That old belle of the morgue.'

'I'm sure a week will be soon enough for us,' Manton remarked. 'I'll let the coroner know the position.'

'So shall I,' Dr. Ryman replied briskly, and charged out of the mortuary like a fretful camel.

Manton looked at his watch. 'A quarter-past nine. I wonder,' he went on in a slowly thoughtful tone, 'just where Susan was this time yesterday evening. That's what we've got to find out next. I think, Dick, we might go visiting the nightspots. What were the names of those two places Neale gave us?'

'The Green Spiral and the Water Mill.'

'Saturday night won't be a bad time either for hawking round that photograph of him and the girl. If I know anything, the places will be packed and we shouldn't have much difficulty finding someone who remembers Susan.'

CHAPTER NINE

George Andrews and his wife sat in silence in the living-room of their cottage. An evening paper lay on his lap though he made no pretence at reading it, and he merely stared for long fixed periods at different points on the wall in front of him. His wife was trying to turn the cuffs on one of his shirts, but frequently had to pause as her eyes brimmed with tears and she was overcome by violent trembling. At a time when each needed to be fortified, it seemed that neither knew how to extend any comfort to the other. Theirs was not so much a sharing of grief as an individual participation, and each felt helpless at this moment to do anything about it.

It was Saturday evening—George Andrews felt he had already lived a hundred years during that Saturday—the evening of the week when, after staying in the garden till darkness made further work impossible, he normally read the evening paper, listened to the radio a bit—he preferred it to television—and generally relaxed until his wife announced that supper was ready. She, on the other hand, always chose Saturday evenings to throw herself into a frenzy of baking cakes and pies and filling the cottage with exquisite smells.

And if Susan had been at home, she for

certain would have been watching television. In his mind's eye, George Andrews saw her now, perched on her favourite low stool in front of the set, her eyes gleaming, her lips slightly parted. Occasionally, she would sigh or a flicker of a smile would pass across her face. Sometimes she would frown or look incredulous, but always her expression would be alive. Never had he seen her sunk in anything like a moronic torpor before the wretched set, or at any other time for that matter.

He quickly focused his attention on a different piece of wall when the picture in his mind's eye became too painful. It was difficult to comprehend that someone as alive as Susan could now be dead. He now switched his gaze to the mantelpiece and frowned. 'What's happened to Susan's photograph?'

His wife winced and closed her eyes. 'It's in the drawer,' she managed to whisper.

'Why?'

'Because I couldn't bear to go on seeing her up there on the mantelpiece.' She looked across at her husband through swollen lids. 'Please, George, leave it in the drawer, just for a few days.'

He turned his head away from her and resumed his silent study of the wall. Perhaps it *was* a good idea not to be so poignantly reminded of Susan. The photograph had been taken only four months before on the eve of her sixteenth birthday. It showed her warm and vital and, there was no getting away from it, provocatively attractive. At that time her hair had been in a pony tail though she never wore it the same for two months on end. God, how proud of her he was! He became aware that his wife was saying something.

'Supposing they never catch the man who did it! I don't think I could continue to live not knowing who . . . who . . .' The sentence petered out in a choking sob.

'Of course they'll find him.' There was a touch of old professional pride in his voice. 'They'll spare no effort to make an arrest, but give them a chance.'

'Do you think it could have been someone in the village?' she asked with anguish.

'I don't know.' A determined look came into his eyes. 'I'm still certain, though, that Christine is holding something back. The Yard officers will have to get the truth out of her.'

'Couldn't you phone through and ask what they've found out so far?'

'I'll get in touch with them in the morning. Not fair to bother them tonight. And anyway they're probably out making inquiries. You don't solve cases by sitting about in police stations.'

'I keep on wondering what he . . . he . . . did to her first.'

'It didn't look as though she'd been raped. I've already told you that, so don't let your imagination run wild.'

'How can I help it! Susan lying strangled in a ditch and you say don't imagine things.'

He had thought it wiser not to tell his wife that a button appeared to have been torn off Susan's blouse, though he had mentioned that her shoes were missing. He was glad now that he hadn't given her the more sinister piece of information.

'We owe it to Susan,' he said stiffly, 'not to imagine things which didn't happen.'

'She was always such a good girl,' she sobbed.

'We both know that. She was the best daughter any parents could have had.'

As he spoke, he forgot his wife's presence and his thoughts were once more only of Susan, *his* daughter. Half an hour later, he got up out of his chair and stared bleakly about the room.

'It's time we went up to bed.'

'I shan't be able to sleep.'

'The doctor left you something for that. Remember, he said you oughtn't to be up at all. Anyway, we're both thoroughly exhausted.'

Winnie Andrews looked appealingly at her husband. 'Oh, George, what are we going to do without Susan?'

'Come on, that's enough of that,' he said, not unkindly, putting an arm round her waist.

Slowly he steered her from the room and up the narrow staircase. She was so forlorn, so pathetically bedraggled, and he became suddenly aware of a faint protective ache stirring uneasily within him.

But it was nothing to the ache he felt for Susan.

★　　　★　　　★

Lady Neale had become so absorbed in writing her speech for the forthcoming general meeting of the Women's Institute that she had lost all sense of time. And what was worse, when she did become aware of it, it was to realise that she hadn't set eyes on her son since those two police officers had called to see him. She hurried out of the drawing-room, across the hall and into the study. It was empty. How curious that he hadn't been to look for her and tell her what it was all about after they had gone. But perhaps he hadn't wanted to disturb her in the throes of composition.

She admitted to herself that she hadn't much cared for the attitude of the two officers. It wasn't that they had been rude, just quietly rock-like. She felt that there would have been no question of intimidating them, not that she would ever admit to trying to intimidate anyone. Persuade and charm, certainly; icily reprove if occasion demanded; but intimidate never. And yet this was the very characteristic a great number of her acquaintances would have been quick to pin on her if their view had been sought.

She ran up the stairs and gave a quick formal knock on her son's bedroom door before bursting in. He was lying on his back on the bed, staring sightlessly at the ceiling.

'Oh, here you are, darling,' Lady Neale exclaimed, a trifle out of breath from her exertions. 'I looked for you in the study. What on earth did those two policemen want? They looked just like characters out of one of those dreadful TV serials you're always watching.' She gave an indulgent laugh. 'Has someone you know got into trouble? Is that what they came about?'

Slowly Michael Neale turned his head. His expression caused his mother to discard the further bright observations which were forming on her lips.

'What's happened, darling? What's the matter?'

He made a small gesture as though to indicate that she was intruding on his thoughts and looked away again. For a few seconds Lady Neale gazed at him with a puzzled expression; then, giving him an eighteen-carat compassionate smile, she perched herself on the side of the bed and seized one of his hands in hers.

'You're worried about something, darling! Tell me what's wrong. I can probably help you. I've always been able to in the past, haven't I?'

'It's nothing, Mother. Honestly, it's nothing,' he said in a weary tone.

Her smile became tender and sad as she went on, 'Do you remember how when you were a little boy and something had gone wrong, you used to run up to your room and hide? And when I came up to find out what it was all about, you'd tell me what had happened and then have a good cry and feel better.' In a wistful tone she added, 'That wasn't all that long ago, you know.' She gave a little false laugh. 'I'm not suggesting you have a good cry now, but I do suggest you let me help you. A trouble shared is a trouble halved, remember.'

His hand as she squeezed it was unresponsive; his face, which never had much colour at the best of times, now looked waxen; his lips had an almost purple tinge and his forehead shone clammily. She rested the back of her hand against his cheek for a second, then with a look of sudden determination she got up from the bed. 'I'm going to send for the doctor.'

He wrenched his head round. 'I don't need the doctor. I'm not ill.'

'Then what is wrong with you?' she demanded.

He bit his lip. 'I've had a bit of a shock,' he said painfully. 'I'll get over it. I'd just like to be left alone.'

'A shock over what, darling?'

'It's something private. I've promised not to talk about it.' He observed his mother's wavering expression. 'It's something affecting a friend.'

'I still think you'd feel happier if you told me about it and got it off your chest,' Lady Neale said in a tone which now held a note of disapproval.

He conjured up a wan smile for her. 'Just leave me. I'll be all right.'

Giving a small shrug to indicate she had done everything which a reasonable mother could, she departed. She arrived back in the drawing-room just as her husband was switching off the radio.

'Hello, dear, I've just been listening to the news. That Susan something-or-other in the village whom Michael once knew has been found strangled in a ditch.' In sudden alarm he went on, 'What on earth's the matter, Grace? You look as though you've just seen a ghost.'

       ★   ★   ★

In common with millions of others in two continents, Bernard Kingston could not help wondering, as he reached out to switch off the television, why Hamilton Burger and Lieutenant Tragg bothered to pit their wits each week against Perry Mason. Would their zeal and tenacity never flag? Would they never lose heart? Kingston hoped not, just as he also hoped they would never win a case.

Grinning at his daughters, he said heartily, 'That's it, kids, Perry's gone off to rest on his laurels till next Saturday and it's time *you* went off to bed. Kiss your father good night and up you go.'

Sylvia and Deirdre Kingston obediently presented their cheeks and received a noisy kiss apiece, also a friendly pat on the behind.

'You've got a spot on your chin, Sylvia. Ask Mummy to put something on it.'

Sylvia scowled while Deirdre, rubbing her cheek in a disdainful manner, said, 'Your moustache always prickles so.'

'You'll like moustaches one day,' her father replied archly.

'I bet I shan't.'

'And what about that scratch on your cheek?' Sylvia now asked.

'Well? What about it?'

'It looks much worse than the spot on my chin.'

'Yes, much,' Deirdre contributed.

'That's enough. Off to bed, both of you. And don't forget to say good night to Mummy. She's in the kitchen, I think.'

'Mummy always comes and says good night to us upstairs,' Sylvia said in a meaning tone.

'I'll come and smack your bottoms upstairs if you don't hurry up,' he replied crossly.

He didn't like to be reproached by his daughters for not giving them as much attention as did their mother; nor to be reminded so bluntly that his bouts of jocularity were not regarded as a substitute for steady affection.

Five minutes later, his wife stuck her head round the door.

'I'm just going up to tuck the girls in.' She hesitated a second. 'You're not going out again this evening, are you?'

He sucked at his moustache and appeared to deliberate for a while. 'Well, I had thought I might slip round to the local for a pint. I promised Fred I'd look in. Saturday night, you know!' he added with a silly grin. 'You've no objections, have you? Shan't be long.'

Peggy Kingston shook her head. 'No,' she said dully. 'I don't mind.'

'I shan't be gone above half an hour,' he said in a falsely bright tone. 'What are you so busy doing out in the kitchen, anyway? You missed Perry.'

'Deirdre's got some friends coming in for tea tomorrow. I was just making a few things for them.'

'All on your lonesome in the kitchen on a Saturday night!' he observed heartily.

'I've got the radio.' She wiped her hands down the front of her apron. As she turned to go back to the kitchen, she said, 'Incidentally, there was something on the news about a girl having been found murdered at Offing.'

Her husband who was straightening his tie in the mirror over the fireplace suddenly froze in his movements. 'What was that?' he called out.

'What?' Her voice floated back from the kitchen.

He walked with studied care across to the door. 'You said something about Offing?' he said, doing his best to sound casual.

'I said that a girl had been found murdered there. It was on the news.'

'What?' he asked, leaning gently against the door. 'What was the name of the girl?'

'I can't remember, I'm afraid.'

Bernard Kingston expelled his breath in a slow hiss. He felt as a man does when he runs up a flight of stairs and reaches the top one step earlier than he had expected. The whole body receives a sudden disagreeable jolt and the recipient automatically pauses to check whether more serious damage has been incurred.

It was a thoughtful and distinctly jittery Bernard Kingston who slipped out of the house a few minutes later and made not for the local but for a newspaper kiosk.

CHAPTER TEN

The Green Spiral and the Water Mill proved to be almost identical establishments in everything but name. Each was a one storey barn-like structure of neo-Tudor design with an outdoor swimming pool at one side. Within, each boasted a cocktail bar with a rather boudoir atmosphere and a large dining-room with floor-space for dancing, and on a dais at the far end from the entrance a small group of apparently unflagging musicians thumped out tunes with a mixture of bored and dedicated expressions.

At the Green Spiral, the waiters were dressed in short green jackets which managed to look crisply chic in the half-light of the restaurant. The waiters of the Water Mill, however, wore powder-blue blazers, which in the brighter lights of that establishment could be seen to be less than orchid fresh.

Manton and Avis had no difficulty in finding someone at each place who remembered having seen Susan and Michael Neale, though their most recent visit which anyone could recollect had been around six weeks before. This came from the hat-check girl at the Water Mill.

'I remember them quite well,' she said. 'They were always rather sweet together. She used to look all excited, and he would fuss quietly about her as though she was his first date. He always gave the impression of being a bit shy.' She raised an eyebrow in an expression of cynical disillusionment. 'But I don't pretend to be a judge of character any more. I've been proved wrong too many times. Tell me she was a little tart and him a gigolo's apprentice, and I'd believe you.' Her expression softened, 'But I'll be sorry to.'

'About how many times have you seen them here?' Manton asked quickly, not being disposed to give the girl an opportunity of telling them the story of her disillusionment with life, which he knew she was eager to do.

'They used to come quite often once, but the last occasion they were here, six weeks ago, was the first time I'd seen them since Christmas.'

'Notice any difference in them?'

'In what sort of way?'

'In any way.'

She frowned in thought. 'No, I don't think so, except perhaps she seemed to take him a bit more for granted than when they first used to come. But that might be my imagination; anyway, she still looked a nice, wholesome girl.'

'You've never seen her here with anyone else?'

'No.' Her glance flitted between them. 'All these questions you're asking, has anything happened to her then?'

'She's been murdered.'

She let out a gasp. 'Murdered! Not by him?'

'We don't know yet who did it.'

'He could never have killed anyone. He was far too nice. He was gentle, too.'

'A possible gigolo's apprentice?' Manton put in unkindly.

'You know I didn't mean that.'

'But you were right, you can't judge anyone by appearances.' He made to put on his hat. 'Thanks for your help, dear.' Taking a final look through to the restaurant, he added, 'Not as busy for a Saturday night as I'd have expected.'

'It's that new place which opened last night, I reckon they've taken a lot of our custom. Probably only temporarily, you know what people are, particularly the sort who use these places. Always for trying somewhere new.'

'Where's this new place?'

'About three miles down the road towards London. It's called the Yellow Caravan. You can't miss it if you're thinking of going there, it's lit up like a film set.'

'And it opened only last night?' Manton asked with interest.

'Yes. Some foreign fellow's running it,' she said scornfully. 'And here am I, who's lived in this country for the whole of my life and I'm just a hat-check girl. Mind you, I'm not against all foreigners. Matter of fact, I'm married to one, he's the wine waiter here. But that's a bit different isn't it?'

Manton and Avis hastily agreed that it was and made their departure. A few minutes later they were being helped out of their car by a commissionaire dressed as a coachman in bright yellow.

'Just leave the car there, sir, and I'll have it parked for you,' he said with a lordly air. 'You have reservations?'

'Any number of them,' Sergeant Avis replied with a dead-pan expression as they pushed their way toward the main entrance.

The Yellow Caravan was certainly packed, and it was some time before they were able to claim anyone's attention. At length Manton managed to button-hole a short, perspiring man in a palm-beach dinner jacket who was bustling around flashing anxious glassy smiles to his right and left.

'I'm afraid if you have no reservation, sir . . .'

'Forget about reservations. I just want you to look at a photograph and tell me whether you recognise either of the persons in it.'

The little man's eyebrows shot up in outraged surprise.

'We're police,' Manton added quietly.

'Police! For goodness' sake, be careful or someone'll hear.'

Followed in more leisurely fashion by

Manton and Avis he scampered across to a door marked PRIVATE and dived into a small office. 'Yes, now, what is it?' he asked testily. Manton produced the photograph which the little man glanced at cursorily.

'Well?' Manton asked.

'My dear officer, if you're asking me whether either of these two young people were at our opening last night, I can't begin to answer. Do you realise there were over two hundred and fifty people here? I wouldn't even have recognised Elizabeth Taylor if she'd walked in.'

'No need to exaggerate,' Avis said.

The little man glared and darted impatient glances about the room. Suddenly he dived to a drawer and pulled out a bundle of photographs.

'If you care to look through these, you may do so, I suppose,' he said doubtfully. 'They were taken last night and must include over half our diners who were here.' He let the photographs drop on to the desk. 'I must ask you to excuse me, but please don't leave before I come back.'

He hurried out of the room and Manton and Avis turned their attention to the pile of photographs. There must have been fifty or sixty of them, all flashlight photographs with a high gloss and showing the previous evening's revellers in various degrees of enjoyment. Most of them were wearing fancy head-dresses and their expressions ranged from toothily cheerful to the downright glum.

'Isn't this Susan?' Avis asked in a tone of sudden excitement, as he pounced on one of the photographs.

Manton stared at it hard. 'Yes, I think it is,' he said slowly. 'I'm sure it is. She might be anything between fifteen and twenty-five in this, but you're right, it definitely is Susan.'

The photograph at which they were looking was of a couple at their table. Their heads were together and the man's right arm was pulling the girl into his side. The girl was smiling shyly into the camera while the man was ogling it relentlessly. He had black hair and appeared swarthy. But his most prominent characteristic was a heavy moustache. As Manton continued to study the photograph, he licked his lips with all the satisfaction of a tom-cat feeling especially replete.

'This is a break,' he crowed. 'Let's go and find little . . . Oh, here he is now.'

'Any use?'

'Yes. Remember seeing this couple by any chance?'

The manager took the photograph and pursed his lips.

'Can't pretend I do, but I see they were at table 46, and I can get hold of their waiter if that'd be any help.'

'It would indeed,' Manton agreed.

The waiter was a thin, wiry man of

middle-age who remembered the couple very well, firstly because he thought the man looked old enough to be the girl's father, though he quickly added that such a sight wasn't unusual in places like the Yellow Caravan; and secondly the man had under-tipped him. Though again he had added that this had come as no surprise. 'You get to know 'em in this game,' he added, for Manton's benefit. He remembered that each had had the mixed grill and that the man, after a prolonged study of the wine list, had ordered the cheapest of the sweet white wines. He told the officers that they had left early, soon after ten.

Though he had heard the man address the girl as Susan, he was not otherwise able to offer any clue as to their identity.

Manton, however, was well satisfied. He had already learnt much more than he'd hoped when they stepped across the garish threshold of the Yellow Caravan.

CHAPTER ELEVEN

George Andrews was wakened from a drugged sleep by the ringing of the telephone down in the hall. As he struggled out of bed, he noticed that he had been in it less than an hour and that it wasn't yet eleven o'clock, despite the sensation that he had just been yanked out of a Rip Van Winkle state of unconsciousness. He immediately recognised Manton's voice on the line and did no more than utter the single monosyllable 'yes' to the request that they might come round and see him straightaway. By the time they arrived he had pulled on a pair of trousers and a thick, roll-neck sweater over the top of his pyjamas.

'I'm sorry to come barging in at this hour,' Manton said, 'but this is something which can't wait till morning.' He motioned Sergeant Avis to pass him the photograph. 'Is that your daughter Susan?'

A muscle twitched at the corner of Andrews's jaw as he stared at the photograph with fascinated gaze.

'Yes,' he said, after a long pause.

'And the man with her?'

'It looks like one of the sales representatives at Yander's, a man named Kingston.'

'Excellent,' Manton remarked. 'I thought it was a less than fifty-fifty chance that you'd be able to identify the man.'

'Where was this taken?' Andrews's voice was thick.

'At a road-house called the Yellow Caravan about twelve miles from here. They had their opening last night.' Andrews's mouth set in a hard line as Manton went on. 'As you've probably guessed, your daughter never went to the school dance at all. Christine was covering up for her.'

Andrews tightened his grip on the back of the chair he was standing behind as Manton asked, 'Had you any idea that your daughter knew this man?'

'I certainly did not.'

'Any idea where he might have met her?'

'Susan has been to a few parties at the factory. The last one was at Christmas. She must have met him then. I remember she danced with a number of different men on that occasion. They had a lot of Paul Joneses and the like to get the thing going.'

Manton scratched the back of his head. 'Next thing is how can we find out where Kingston lives? Find out *now*, that is?'

'I can ring the night guard. They have a list of addresses of all employees at the gate.'

'Just before you do, you are certain that that *is* Kingston in the photograph?'

Andrews gave it a further careful scrutiny. 'Yes, I'm sure it is.'

'Fine, then as soon as we know his address, we'll go and see him. Incidentally, does he live in the village?'

Andrews shook his head as he left to go and telephone. 'In one of the London suburbs, I think.'

While he was out of the room, Manton said quietly to Avis, 'No need to tell him the whole story yet. Let him get over this shock first.'

'You mean you're not going to tell him about Susan and Michael Neale?'

Manton nodded. 'More particularly that she mayn't have been a virgin.'

Andrews came back into the room. 'Kingston's address is 64 Colefax Avenue, Woodford. He's the sales rep. for Hertfordshire and Essex.'

'It's going to take us over an hour to get there, even at this time of night,' Manton observed as they prepared to leave.

★   ★   ★

By the time that Manton had reported to his headquarters, which had been temporarily set up in Offing Police Station, and asked that a message should be transmitted to J Division of the Metropolitan Police, in which area Colefax Avenue lay, it was near enough half-past eleven. Leaving Detective-Sergeant Hay in drowsy command, Manton, Sergeant Avis and Detective-Inspector Donald of the local force set off for Woodford, where they arrived seventy-five minutes later.

Colefax Avenue, a street of detached modern villas, was silent and dark as they drove slowly along it, looking for number 64. An occasional light showed in an upstairs room and two cats suddenly streaked across their path, but otherwise there was no sign of life.

'I always feel like the ruddy Gestapo when I knock on doors at this hour,' Manton said in a tone of self-disgust as they parked and got out.

'Don't forget, sir, we're after a murderer. That's the difference.'

When the front door of No. 64 opened, none of the officers had any difficulty in recognising the man who stood before them as the same man who had leered into the camera at the Yellow Caravan the previous night.

'We're police officers,' Manton announced. 'We'd like to have a word with you, Mr. Kingston. May we come in?'

Kingston, unshaven and tousle-headed, gazed at them with alarm. 'Can't you wait till the morning, whatever it is?' he asked in an agitated voice.

'It's too urgent.' Manton cocked his head on one side. 'Perhaps you'd prefer to come along to the station?'

'Good grief, what an alternative! All right, then, come into the dining-room. I'll just slip upstairs and tell my wife.'

Manton and Avis exchanged glances, and then Avis followed Kingston up the stairs, to the latter's obvious consternation.

'It's all right,' Avis hissed. 'I won't come into the bedroom, but don't shut the door.'

A short, whispered colloquy went on inside the bedroom of which Avis was unable to hear more than an occasional word. Indeed, the only word he did clearly recognise and which was repeated several times was 'police'. When Kingston emerged from the bedroom, he had brushed his hair and re-knotted his dressing-gown.

'I must say I didn't know this happened outside of movies,' he remarked with a sickly grin, as he and Avis rejoined the other two.

'You obviously don't read the newspapers,' Manton replied in sardonic tone.

Then for several seconds the two men stared at each other in silence. Manton realised that the interview was crucial and it was vitally important that he shouldn't mishandle it. At this moment everything pointed to Bernard Kingston being the girl's murderer. The next few minutes were going to confirm or destroy this suspicion.

'I understand you knew Susan Andrews?' he said, watching Kingston closely.

'Yes, I've met her. Her father is security officer with the firm I work for.' He shook his head slowly. 'Terrible thing about her death, I saw it in the stop-press.'

'Have you seen her recently?' Manton asked. Let him lie about that, he thought, and I've as good as got him.

'Seen her recently,' Kingston repeated, nervously massaging one of his fingers. 'As a matter of fact I have. I . . . er . . . saw her yesterday.'

Manton experienced a faint sense of anti-climax. He could only presume Kingston had realised that his visit to the Yellow Caravan could be traced. He probably remembered the photograph being taken.

'Where was that?' he asked.

'Well, as a matter of fact, I took her out to dinner last night.'

'And after that?'

'I took her home; not late, about half-past ten. She said she'd promised her parents not to be late.'

'Did you take her right back to her front door?'

'Almost.'

'What do you mean by that?'

'I dropped her at the end of the lane in which she lives.'

'Why?'

Kingston gave them a sheepish grin. 'She didn't want her parents to see the car.'

'How old are you?' Manton's voice was steely.

'Thirty-six.'

'And you're married?'

'Yes.'

'With children?'

'Two girls.'

For a second Kingston looked puzzled but he quickly flushed when Manton asked, 'Do you often take sixteen-year-olds out for the evening?' It was not a very useful question but he felt better for asking it.

'I didn't know she was only sixteen,' Kingston blustered. 'And anyway she came of her own free will. She didn't have to go out with me if she didn't want to.'

'You realise you were the last person to see her alive?' Manton asked.

'The person who killed her saw her after me.'

'I believe you were that person. I believe you murdered her.'

Bernard Kingston's jaw sagged and his eyes looked as though they might pop out. He struggled to find words. 'I murder her! You're bluffing. Of course I didn't. I'm not a sex maniac.'

'Who said anything about sex maniacs?'

'Well, wasn't it one of them who killed her? It usually is with girls found strangled in ditches.'

'How did you get that scratch on your face?'

Manton had the impression that the change of tack brought Kingston relief.

'A cat did it. Well, a kitten actually.' With an obvious return of confidence he went on, 'I'd probably better start at the beginning and tell you the whole story of last night. I took Susan out to dinner at the Yellow Caravan, as I've already mentioned, but quite frankly the evening wasn't a great success. She seemed ill at ease most of the time and after we'd had a couple of dances she wanted to go home, so . . .' He gave an expressive shrug to indicate his views on the caprices of the opposite sex. 'So leave we did. We drove straight back and I dropped her at the end of the lane leading to her home. And *that* was the last I saw of her.'

'What time was that?'

'I've told you, about half-past ten.'

'You make it sound very innocent, don't you?' Manton remarked caustically.

'It *was* very innocent.'

'Men your age don't take out sixteen-year-old girls whom they scarcely know for innocent purposes. You won't persuade me your intentions were all that pure. And, anyway, apart from your own word, what proof is there of what you say? It strikes me as much more likely that after you left the Yellow Caravan you drove on to Offing airfield for a quiet necking session, in the course of which you strangled her because she wouldn't give in to you.'

Kingston bared his teeth in an unattractive grimace. 'Pure imagination and you haven't any evidence because there couldn't be any. Before you made that wild charge, you asked what proof there was that I was telling the truth. Well, I have got proof if you're prepared to listen for a minute.

'After I'd dropped Susan and was driving along the road which runs at the back of

Yander's factory, I suddenly saw a friend standing at the roadside—Fred Crowland, you'd better make a note of his name—he's a sales representative same as I am. He'd been working late in preparation for a meeting yesterday, and when he came to leave he couldn't get his car to start, so he was hoping to thumb a lift. He lives about five miles from Offing. I picked him up and drove him home, and went in for a drink. And that was when I got this scratch. He has a new kitten and it took a dislike to my face.'

'What time did you arrive back here?'

'I can't remember. Some time after midnight, it would have been.'

There was a silence and then Manton said, 'Of course you could still have murdered Susan. This Fred Crowland doesn't provide you with an alibi. We don't know the exact time of Susan's death, it could have been before you met Crowland.'

Kingston's confident look melted. 'I tell you I had nothing to do with her death and you can't prove that I did.'

Manton gave an abstracted nod as though the denial was no more than an expected formality. 'Tell me,' he said, 'how much of all this does your wife know?'

'She doesn't know I was out with Susan,' he said with an embarrassed air. 'She thinks I was out with some men friends.'

'I see.'

'I hope you won't . . . well, won't upset her.'

'By telling her that you weren't? No, I won't tell her the truth—not yet, anyway.'

Leaving Kingston looking as though he'd been receiving visitors from another planet, they departed.

It was two o'clock on Sunday morning, an hour at which even the vitality of police officers is low. Manton yawned and rubbed his eyes as they returned to the car. 'I suppose we might as well go to bed for a few hours.'

Detective-Inspector Donald, who had been wearing a somewhat worried expression since the end of the interview, now said, 'You don't think, Mr. Manton, that we had enough to take in Kingston straight away?'

'Do you?' Manton asked, without enthusiasm.

'He was the last person to be seen with the girl, and as you pointed out yourself, sir, his so-called alibi isn't one.'

'Nevertheless, I'd like to see the case against him strengthened before we pull him in. He won't run away, and the next day or so should help us to close a few of the gaps.' He turned to Avis. 'Make a note to check with C.R.O., Dick, whether our friend has any form; also to send somebody along first thing in the morning to go over his car.'

Manton realised that the local officer was

probably branding him as super-cautious, if not timorous, but the responsibility for making an arrest was his and not Inspector Donald's. It wouldn't be the inspector who would be grilled—publicly at that—if a charge which was made on insufficient evidence later suffered fatal erosive processes. Give him four or five hours sleep now and he'd be ready in the morning to put Kingston's story under the microscope, piece by piece. Let it show a crack at almost any point and there might be enough to justify charging him with Susan's murder.

They had been on the case less than twelve hours: a case which had started with a body in a ditch and no suspect in view. Now, however, the worst was over. No longer were they working in the dark.

CHAPTER TWELVE

As soon as the door was opened and he had announced his identity it was apparent to Manton that Fred Crowland was a very nervous person. He was holding a napkin in his hand and immediately began to whisk it about his legs.

'I'm afraid I'm still having my breakfast,' he said, with an anxious smile. 'I'm always a bit late on Sunday mornings.'

'We can talk to you while you finish your breakfast,' Manton said pleasantly. 'Half-past nine on a Sunday morning isn't the best hour to receive callers.'

Crowland fluttered the napkin at an insect. 'The whole place is in a bit of a mess. I haven't even shaved yet. I live on my own, you see.'

He led the way into a room and began to remove magazines and worn-looking newspapers which appeared to cover most of the chairs.

'I see you have a kitten,' Manton remarked with interest.

'Oh . . . er . . . ah . . . yes.'

'Bit of a tie keeping a pet, isn't it, living on your own?'

'It'll be company for when I get home,' he said in a far from happy tone.

Sergeant Avis put out a hand and scooped the kitten off the chair and held it up against his cheek. The kitten closed its eyes and purred ecstatically.

'Careful he doesn't scratch you,' Crowland exclaimed.

'Has he ever scratched anyone?' Manton asked in an apparently casual tone.

'Yes, a friend of mine the other evening.'

'Mr. Kingston?'

Crowland nodded, at the same time giving the impression of someone entering the firing line. However, in the ensuing period of question and answer, he supported Kingston's account of his movements.

'How did Mr. Kingston strike you when he picked you up on Friday evening?' Manton asked.

'Just his normal self.'

'Not tense or upset?'

'No.'

'Or frightened?'

'Definitely not.'

Which is more than can be said for you, my friend, Manton thought to himself. If you're telling the truth, what are you so agitated about?

'Did he tell you where he had been?'

'I believe he said he'd been out to dinner with someone. I didn't really listen.'

'Have you ever heard him mention the name of Susan Andrews?'

Crowland put on a worried frown. 'Susan Andrews? Susan Andrews? . . . No, I don't think I have.'

Manton noticed that after each answer Crowland threw him an anxious look as though to check the reaction to what he had said. It now seemed to Manton that no further progress would be made without a frontal assault and this he decided to launch.

'Has Mr. Kingston been in touch with you since Friday evening?'

'No.'

'Quite sure, Mr. Crowland?' Manton asked in a steely voice.

Crowland swallowed and looked wildly around the room as if expecting it to dematerialise. He gave an energetic nod.

'You're quite sure that Mr. Kingston hasn't asked you to give false evidence on his behalf?'

'Definitely not.' The denial emerged in an explosive stammer.

'O.K., Mr. Crowland, we'll doubtless be seeing you again later.'

As they rose to go, Sergeant Avis said silkily, 'I wouldn't ring Mr. Kingston as soon as we've left. He's probably sleeping late. He had rather a disturbed night.'

They went out into the hall and Manton was on the point of opening the front door when it received a series of thunderous knocks.

'More Sunday morning visitors?' he remarked, as he opened it.

On the step stood two small girls with expressions of comical surprise at being confronted by a pair of strange faces.

'Where's Uncle Fred Crowland?' The larger one asked in a mystified tone. Crowland chose this moment to appear in the hall, and the children dashed in past Manton and Avis.

'Uncle Fred Crowland, Uncle Fred Crowland,' they chorused excitedly, 'where's your new kitten, may we see it?'

Manton's ears pricked with interest. 'How

long have you had the kitten?' he asked.

The children gazed at him in surprise, and in the silence which followed it was the smaller girl who piped up. 'It's one of Mrs. Lusher's kittens. Uncle Fred Crowland fetched it last night. Didn't you?'

Aware that they were the cause of a certain tension, the elder girl now said in a burst of explanation, 'When we went round to see Mrs. Lusher's kittens just now, she said you'd fetched the other one. We hadn't seen them before, you see,' she said earnestly to Manton. 'They were born while we were staying with our auntie in Hastings. We arrived home last night, but Mummy wouldn't let us go round to Mrs. Lusher's until this morning.'

Before Manton could say anything, Crowland blurted out, 'I'm afraid I wasn't quite right just now. The kitten didn't scratch Bernard's face, but he phoned me last night and said he'd told his wife that was how he had come by the scratch and I must back him up.' Crowland gulped noisily. 'He said it was important that I get hold of a kitten right away in case anyone came asking about it. I knew Mrs. Lusher's cat had had a litter recently so I went round to see her and . . . well, this is the kitten.'

Manton was prepared for the moment to accept the gloss which Crowland had given his account. He asked: 'Did you see Kingston at all on Friday evening?'

'Yes, definitely yes. Apart from the untruth about the kitten, everything was exactly as I've told you.'

'Then I assume Kingston already had the scratch on his face when he picked you up?'

'Yes, I think he did,' he said miserably. 'I feel terrible, letting him down this way.'

'He shouldn't have involved you in the first place,' Manton remarked unsympathetically. 'Moreover, it's lucky for you the truth came out when it did or you might have found the wave being taken out of your hair.'

Leaving Crowland making further efforts at excusing himself and the two small girls looking goggle-eyed from one grown-up to another, Manton and Avis departed.

'Looks like we now have enough to put Master Kingston through the wringer,' Manton remarked as they headed in the direction of Offing. 'As to that scratch on his face, what's the betting the laboratory don't find bits of his skin amongst Susan's nail scrapings?'

★   ★   ★

Sunday morning was the time which P.C. Newbold invariably devoted to what the Army is pleased to call interior economy. After pressing his uniform and sponging his helmet with a dilution of cleaning fluid, he would spend half an hour polishing his boots until they outshone any manufacturer's advertisement. This done, he would retire into his small office and check his supplies of stationery, particularly the multitude of official forms. Next came his round of the notice-boards; obsolete notices would be removed and replaced by the latest batch relating to wanted criminals, lost property, missing persons and the annual arrival of the Colorado beetle.

On this particular Sunday morning, however, routine had gone by the board and Offing Police Station resembled the communications centre of a summit meeting. Manton had insisted that he must have his operational headquarters on the spot, however physically inconvenient.

'The village is the place where we're going to get information,' he had said, 'so let everyone know they've only to step down the street in order to give it.'

And this Sunday morning did in fact bring its visitors to Offing Police Station, amongst them Captain Walter Armstrong, who arrived a few minutes before Manton and Avis returned from their visit to Crowland.

One of the young detective-constables, who had been drafted into Offing for the occasion, button-holed Sergeant Avis as he entered the station. 'He says he's got important information . . . wouldn't tell me what it was, said he'd only speak to the Scotland Yard men . . .'

'O.K. I'll see him,' Avis replied briskly, and a minute later found himself confronted by a tall, stern-faced individual with thin lips and a long nose of purplish hue. He was wearing a cap and well-polished brown leggings; somehow the rest of his clothing didn't make any impression on Avis.

'I'm Detective-Sergeant Avis, I understand you have some information to give . . .'

'Are you a local officer?'

'No, I'm from the Yard.'

Armstrong gave a satisfied grunt. 'Good! Most of the local police are idiots, just a waste of time talking to them. Go to the man in charge, that's what I always say.'

Avis let this go. Armstrong was clearly a peppery customer and the less said the sooner he was likely to come to the point.

'My name's Armstrong, *Captain* Armstrong. I own a riding stable a mile out of the village, have about half a dozen horses. Give riding lessons to the sons and daughters of the local gentry, that sort of thing.'

Avis maintained an interested expression, though he couldn't help reflecting that the sons and daughters referred to must find their lessons something of an ordeal.

Captain Armstrong looked around him with distaste and went on, 'About this girl who's been found strangled up on the airfield, I saw her on Friday night.'

Avis started. 'When?'

'Between half-past eleven and midnight, nearer midnight probably.'

'Are you sure it was as late as that?'

'Certain.'

'And where did you see her?'

'Do you know this district?'

'Not very well.'

'Do you know where Langdale Farm is?' Avis shook his head. 'Well, it's about a couple of miles from here.'

'In the direction of the airfield?'

'No.'

'Of Yander's factory then?'

'No, it's nowhere near either of them. But that's where I saw her, about half a mile this side of Langdale Farm and walking in the direction of Offing.'

'And you're sure it was Susan Andrews?'

Captain Armstrong looked at Avis as though he had committed some hideous equestrian misdemeanour. 'Of course I'm sure. I wouldn't have taken the trouble to come along here if I hadn't been sure. I had my headlights full on and I could identify her quite clearly.'

'Did she make an attempt to attract your attention?'

Armstrong's mouth twitched. 'Yes, she did,' he said with a detectable note of defiance in his voice.

'But you didn't stop?'

'No, I didn't.'

'May I ask why you didn't?' Avis inquired with curiosity.

'Because I don't believe in picking up girls late at night.'

'But you knew who she was.'

'All the more reason in this instance for not stopping.'

Avis stared at him in astonishment. 'What are you trying to say?'

'I'm simply saying that I don't give late-night lifts in my car to girls like Susan Andrews. However, I didn't come here to discuss my principles, but to give you information. Unless you have anything further you wish to ask me about it, I'll go.'

Avis gave his head a puzzled shake. 'I'm afraid I must pursue this,' he said, meeting Armstrong's hard stare. 'What do you know about Susan Andrews to make you say that?'

'Ask someone else.'

'I'm asking you. You made the remark.'

'Well, if your inquiries haven't already disclosed what sort of a girl she was, they soon will. I haven't myself read *Lolita*, but Susan Andrews was of the same ilk as the heroine of that story.'

'You mean she was a nymphomaniac?'

'I mean,' Armstrong replied with tight-lipped severity, 'that she was far too interested in the opposite sex for a girl of her age.'

'Did she ever bother you?'

'No. But I never gave her a chance.'

'Was there any indication she might have if you had?'

Armstrong shrugged. 'Don't ask me, I don't know! But if you want to find out more about her, speak to Lady Neale at Offing Hall. She had the unhappy experience of having her son—he's up at Cambridge—pursued by the girl.'

There was something about Armstrong's manner and tone which Avis found tauntingly self-righteous.

'I suppose you realise,' he said, 'that if you *had* stopped for her, she might now be alive?'

'I do, and my visit here is to make some small amend. I didn't have to come forward, and if I hadn't you'd probably never have discovered this particular piece of the jigsaw—if it is a jigsaw—but I felt it was my duty to proffer my piece of information; though, mind you, I'm no less determined not to give late-night lifts to girls.' He rose to his feet. 'Is that all?'

Avis collected his thoughts with difficulty. He really didn't know what to make of the captain. 'Did you notice how she was dressed?'

'A blouse and a skirt, I think.'

'Did she appear dishevelled in any way?'

'Not that I noticed.'

'And she just tried to thumb a lift, is that it?'

'Correct.'

Avis rubbed the tip of his nose. 'I'm very glad you did come forward, Captain Armstrong. I'd just like to get down on paper what you've told me and then that'll be all for the time being.'

Twenty minutes later, when Armstrong had departed, Avis went in search of P.C. Newbold. 'What can you tell me about Captain Armstrong?' he asked, when he had found him.

'Not an easy man to get along with,' Newbold remarked with a reminiscent glint in his eye.

'That much I've gathered. He seems to have deep-rooted suspicion of girls.'

'That's on account of his experience. It was several years ago, before I came to the village, not long after the war in fact. A couple of girls, who lived here in those days, alleged that he regularly used to have intercourse with them in the loft above his stables. Well, even though he strenuously denied it, charges were preferred, and then in the proceedings before the magistrates the girls virtually admitted they'd made it all up out of spite and the case was chucked out.'

'How old were the girls?'

'They were fifteen at the time. It later came out that he'd chased them off his premises with a riding whip one day and wouldn't give back the watch which one of the girls dropped in her flight.'

'It all fits together,' Avis said with a wry smile, 'and explains why he's anti-young girls; also why he still nurses jaundiced feelings against his local police.'

'He certainly doesn't love us! He's always writing to the Chief Constable complaining about one thing or another. Once it was to report me for obstructing a pavement with my bicycle. I'd leant it up against a wall and it had slipped down.'

'Almost sounds as if he's a case. Do you think one should believe what he says about seeing Susan Andrews last night?'

Newbold nodded. 'It would have been much simpler for him to have stayed out of the inquiry, but I think he probably did come forward, as he says, as an amend for not stopping. He's the sort of bloke who would have a conscience about it.'

The door opened and Manton peered into the room. 'Who was that sour-looking beanstalk I saw leaving just now?'

'I was just coming to tell you about him, sir.'

Sergeant Avis gave Manton an account of Armstrong's visit, at the end of which Manton said: 'I want a plan of the area on which we can mark the times at which various people saw Susan at various points. And if I know anything, they'll mostly cancel out,' he added bitterly. 'Incidentally, I've also been interviewing a volunteer of information. A chap who says he saw Michael Neale on Friday night cruising about in his car at the end of the village where the Andrews live: says he noticed him twice between half-past ten and eleven. Each time he was unaccompanied. But the point is Neale told us he spent the evening in London and didn't reach home till after midnight. Frankly, I'd like to know what this informant's after. He was a bit too greasy and I didn't take to him much.' He turned to Newbold. 'Do you know Trevor Caunt?'

'I do indeed, sir. A nasty bit of work, usually trying to make trouble somewhere. He recently served a month for maintenance arrears. Deserted his wife a couple of years ago and moved in with a really low creature who runs the sweet shop, and who's had a number of illegitimate children. Doesn't know who half the fathers are, I often suspect.' He looked suddenly thoughtful. 'Come to think of it, sir, I believe Lady Neale was chairman of the bench when Caunt came up. It was she who sentenced him.'

'It doesn't necessarily mean he's not telling the truth about seeing her son on the night of the murder,' Manton said in a doubtful tone, 'though I still don't like him.'

The three officers looked at each other in a thoughtful silence. Like true love, police investigations seldom maintained a smooth course. Important witnesses would often be in conflict over vital issues, and, in Manton's experience, every case produced at least one feature which obstinately refused to be reconciled with all the others. Having made up his mind in the present instance that Kingston was the prime suspect, it was disconcerting to have Michael Neale's shadow suddenly thrown across the trail. He made a mental note to pump Christine Thrupp again. He reckoned she could probably tell him more about the dead girl than anyone else.

CHAPTER THIRTEEN

When Lady Neale entered her son's bedroom at half-past nine on that same Sunday morning she was surprised to find it empty.

For the past hour she had been in her own room with the door half open and she could have sworn he hadn't left his room. At all events, he must be feeling better. A good night's rest had put him right. That was the trouble with someone as sensitive as Michael, he became so easily upset behind the shy, retiring façade which most people, apart from his mother, took to be his real nature.

Poor boy! Shocked over something affecting a friend! Presumably he had slept on it and was now able to see it in better perspective, just as his mother had overcome her initial shock after being told of Susan Andrews's death. Then, for one awful confusing moment, she had connected that event with her son's abnormal state when he came in the previous evening. But reason had come to her rescue and she had realised what an absurd idea this was. Worse than absurd, it was disloyal. Michael had broken with the girl; he had told her so. And anyway, he had been up in London with friends that evening.

She caught sight of a piece of paper, over on his dressing-table. It was propped against his stud box and she went across the room and picked it up. But even before she had put on her spectacles, she realised it was a note addressed to herself. It read:

Dear Mother,
    Woke up early and decided to go back to Cambridge now to avoid the traffic later in the day. Will phone you one evening this week. Nothing to worry about.

Love,
Michael.

At about the time that his mother was reading the note, Michael Neale was sitting in his car in a lay-by a few miles short of Cambridge. He had left home soon after half-past six and had been parked in the lay-by for the last hour.

He had felt that he had to get away from the cloying atmosphere of home as quickly as possible in order to be able to think. He only prayed that his mother wouldn't rush to phone the college authorities or make any other impetuous move. Perhaps he had better get in touch with her sooner than he'd intended in order to forestall any action she might be contemplating. He also had it in mind to telephone the police within the next hour or so. He didn't want them going up to the house and then jumping to wild conclusions when they found he wasn't there.

Dreamily he moved his left hand and rested it on the short, stumpy gear lever, and was immediately reminded how Susan had loved playing with it, pretending to drive and sometimes actually changing gear under his instruction. With the sharp realisation that she would never again be at his side in the car, he felt hollow and empty as though his whole being was no more than a mummified shell. Suddenly in his mind's-eye he saw her again, her hair flying, her eyes shining with excitement as she urged him to drive ever faster. And then, the journey over, she would rest her head against his shoulder in warm submission and their lips would meet in a kiss which would leave them both panting a little, and tingling all over.

A large pantechnicon swung into the lay-by and parked just ahead of him. The driver climbed out of the cab and walked back to the car. 'Got a light, mate?'

Neale produced a book of matches. 'Not in any trouble, are you?' he asked, through a cloud of noisily expelled smoke.

'No, I'm O.K.'

'Thought you must have broken down or something, sitting here all by yourself.'

'No, I'm just having a quiet think.'

The driver looked at him in alarm. 'Good luck, mate,' he muttered, as he retired to his own vehicle.

Two minutes later Neale had the lay-by to himself and his thoughts again gathered like mourners round Susan's grave. Would he ever be able to forget the stark horror of Friday night, of suddenly seeing Susan lying crumpled and lifeless in that ditch? He was filled now with searing bitterness against the man responsible for her death. How dared he have laid his groping hands on her! It would be almost better never to know who he was.

★　　★　　★

Peggy Kingston poked her head round the living-room door and saw with surprise that her husband was sitting with his feet up turning the pages of the *Sunday Pictorial*.

'I thought I heard you go out just now,' she said. He made no reply and she went on, 'I was almost sure I heard the car being started.'

'You probably did. The police have taken it,' he said bleakly.

'The police! What on earth for?'

Kingston removed his feet off the chair and gave his wife a look of anxious self-pity. 'Come and sit down beside your old man, Peggy. He's in trouble.'

Closing the door, Peggy Kingston pulled out a chair and sat down facing her husband across the table. He looked at her reproachfully. 'I'm not infectious,' he said, with a small, strained smile. 'You could come and sit a bit closer.'

Ignoring his remark, she asked suspiciously, 'What sort of trouble?'

With a martyred sigh he sat back in his chair and buried his chin in the yellow and brown silk scarf which was knotted round his neck. Then carefully avoiding her gaze, he said: 'That girl who was murdered at Offing on Friday night, well I happened to see her that day. And of course the police wanted to know if I could help them with their inquiries.'

'And could you?' she asked quietly.

'Not much, no.'

'Why have they taken the car?'

'Search me, Peggy!' he said in a bluff tone of injured innocence.

'Are you proposing to tell me how you came

to be with this girl on the evening—I assume it was the evening—she was murdered?'

'Peggy!' he said coaxingly, 'you sound just like an iceberg talking. Can't you give your old man a bit of comfort in his hour of need?'

She bit her lip and gazed at him with a worried expression. 'Stop acting like a misjudged schoolboy, Bernard; and if you want my help tell me exactly what happened.'

'Come and sit over here on the arm of my chair,' he said in a wheedling tone, 'and I'll tell you everything.'

'I can hear perfectly well here.'

He gave a long-suffering shrug. 'O.K., Peggy, if you want to rub in the salt, go ahead. But here's the truth! As you know, I had to call at the factory at the end of my rounds on Friday and when I'd finished there, it was about half-past six, so I decided to call at the local in Offing for a pint. When I came out I just happened to run into this girl whom I'd met once or twice before at company socials and . . . Well, I knew you weren't expecting me back for supper, so—'

'Only because you'd said you wouldn't be back,' she broke in. 'You were, if you remember, going out for an evening with the boys.'

'As I was saying,' he went on in a pained tone, 'I knew you weren't expecting me home till bedtime, so on the spur of the moment I suggested we should go and have a bite together. I wasn't with her more than a couple of hours and then I dropped her near her home and drove on back.'

'With your face scratched.'

'I've told you that was Fred's kitten. I called in at Fred's on my way home. I happened to pick him up and give him a lift.'

In the silence which followed, he cast surreptitious glances in his wife's direction. Eventually she spoke and her tone was infinitely weary.

'And now they suspect you of having killed the girl.' It came out more as a statement than as a question.

'Good God, Peggy, don't get all dramatic. They automatically suspect everyone who ever knew her. They're probably eliminating me and lots of others at this very moment.'

'Did they know about . . . about the other time?'

'That's damned unfair, Peggy, throwing that in my face.'

She gave a small shrug. 'Well, what is it you want me to do?'

'That's my girl!' he said, with a quick return of his normally breezy manner. 'But don't make it sound as though I'm going to ask you to commit rank perjury. All I ask you to do is to stick by me.' He gave her a small, sad grin. 'That's not too much for a husband to ask of his wife, is it? I don't know whether the police will be round again, but if they are, all you have to do is stick by your old man and tell them he's not the sort of bloke who commits murders.' In a carefully casual tone, he went on, 'It could be that *times* will play an important part in this case. Frankly, I've no idea what time I got in on Friday night.' He caught and held her eye as he said meaningly, 'But it wasn't very late, was it?'

He rose from his chair and, coming round to his wife's side of the table, rested a hand on her shoulder. 'We've faced our difficulties before, Peggy, and got through together. We'll do it again.'

He drifted out into the hall, leaving his wife staring in mute misery at his empty chair.

★   ★   ★

George Andrews tried not to look at his reflection in the mirror as he knotted his tie and prepared to go out. While he was putting on his jacket, his wife came into the bedroom.

'Oh! You've made the bed,' she said in a surprised tone, which was not unjustified seeing that he had not been known to do so before.

'Yes.'

Why he had made it this particular Sunday morning he couldn't have brought himself to tell her; though, in fact, it was nothing less than a small inarticulate gesture of reconciliation, an unobtrusive proffering of a tiny olive-branch. She said nothing, however, and he was immediately filled with a sense of irritation, watching her as she stood staring vacantly at the bed, dressed in an ill-assortment of wholly black garments. What had she wanted to do that for? You could show your respect for the dead without dressing like a crow. It wasn't even as if she was a particularly religious person. If it wouldn't have been so childishly obvious, he'd have felt inclined to remove his own black tie and put on a coloured one, just to evoke some comment from her which in turn would add fuel to his irritation.

'Are you going out?' she asked, at last.

'I told you I was going up to the police station.'

'You won't be away long, will you?'

'I don't expect so.'

'If anyone calls, shall I tell them where you've gone?'

'Yes, you can if you like.' His tone was deliberately unhelpful.

'I'd like to make arrangements for the funeral this afternoon,' she said with quiet determination.

'You won't be able to. In the first place, I doubt whether you can on a Sunday, and in any event no arrangements can be made until the coroner has given his certificate. I will try and find out about the inquest, however.'

Her expression became more haunted and he could see that she was on the verge of tears. 'I think it's horrible,' she said in a quavering voice, 'keeping her body lying in the mortuary all this time. It isn't human, it's cruel and beastly.'

'Well, there isn't anything we can do about it.' He picked up his wallet off the dressing-table and made for the door. 'I shan't be very long and you know where I am.'

Deciding that walking would provide a better antidote to his feelings than driving the car, he set off on foot. Also he wanted a bit of time to sort out his thoughts before he confronted his one-time colleagues. Only an iron self-discipline had enabled him not to show his stunned incredulity when Manton had shown him the photograph the previous night. The sight of it had knocked him right off-balance so that it had been some time before he could begin to unravel the implications.

What had been hardest of all for him to accept was the fact that Susan had misled him about where she was going that evening. For much of the night he had lain awake trying to find an explanation for her conduct. She had always been truthful and straightforward and he could have sworn that she would never deceive him over anything of substance. And if on this occasion she had done so, it was not difficult to see now where the blame properly lay.

Kingston had obviously played upon her immature emotions and flattered her by his attention. There was a certain brassy panache about the man which, he supposed, might well impress a girl who had led a relatively sheltered life. She must have been temporarily swept away by the so-called sophistication of a man who was old enough to be her father. It was obviously he who had also impressed upon her the need for secrecy, probably making the whole enterprise sound all the more exciting by doing so and apparently overcoming the scruples she must have felt about lying to her parents.

He was filled with bitterness that Fate should have selected his daughter for her victim when so many other girls played with fire with a far more persistent recklessness. Perhaps it was because she had led a more sheltered life than many, that she had failed to recognise danger until it was too late. Danger in the shape of Bernard Kingston!

George Andrews had never given much heed to gossip, but you couldn't work at Yander's for very long without picking up some of the sniggered tales about Don Juan Kingston and his heavily-embellished triumphs with the opposite sex. There's always one to be found in every office and factory, and Bernard Kingston was Yander's ladies' man by popular nomination. Andrews's face was a granite mask as he turned into the police station. Soon he would learn the only thing he wanted to know. Had Kingston been charged yet?

Manton sighed when told that Andrews wished to see him, since he felt reasonably certain that he had come to solicit and not impart information. Also the time must come sooner or later when he would have to learn that his daughter wasn't all she had seemed to be. The two men met in the small cupboard-like space which led off the general office.

'Did you manage to trace Kingston?' Andrews asked as they sat down on opposite sides of a small desk which all but filled the room.

'Yes, we traced him all right.'

'Has he been arrested yet?'

'No. We haven't got enough against him, but I'm pretty sure we shall have before long.'

'Did he admit being out with Susan on Friday night?'

At this point Manton decided to give Andrews the whole story to date. He was, after all, not only the victim's father but an ex-detective-inspector whose discretion could be relied upon.

'There is one other matter I think I should mention to you,' he added, when he had finished describing the interview with Kingston. 'There's a suggestion that your daughter may not have been a virgin at the time of her death.'

He went on to explain Dr. Ryman's findings while Andrew's expression grew more forbidding.

'Does this mean you're going to try and throw mud at my daughter when the case reaches court?' he asked bitingly.

'Of course it doesn't, but I thought you ought to know what the doctor found. And anyway there's no question of throwing mud, there's no suggestion that Susan regularly misconducted herself.'

'There'd better not be either! It'd be a damned lie!' In a tone which carried unmistakable criticism he went on, 'When do you expect to arrest Kingston?'

'I can't say.'

'Why don't you think you've enough against him now? He was the last known person with her, he lied to you about the scratch on his face, and anyone'll tell you he's a recognised womaniser.'

'I don't doubt it, but it's not evidence,' Manton replied evenly. 'Moreover, Captain Armstrong's statement of seeing Susan near Langdale Farm around midnight doesn't tie up—yet.'

'It simply means . . .'

'Yes?'

'That Kingston has lied to an even greater extent than you can yet prove.'

'Perhaps, but I'd like to be in a position to prove it before we arrest him.'

Andrew's gaze flickered round the tiny office before coming to rest again on Manton. In a meaning tone he said, 'I hoped to find you already had him under lock and key.'

'I know how you feel, Mr. Andrews, but give us time. It wouldn't help you if we barged in too soon.'

It was clear, however, that Andrews was in no mood to be persuaded. 'What about the inquest?'

'I was about to mention that, it's eleven o'clock tomorrow. Just formal evidence of identification and cause of death, and then a long adjournment.'

Andrews got up from his chair, 'I'll be there.'

'Will you be having a solicitor watching the proceedings on your behalf?'

'*I'll* be doing that,' he replied tersely, and disappeared through the door.

Manton sighed and returned his attention to the plan of the district he'd been studying when Andrews arrived. Not for the first time he wondered who but a detective would work the whole of Saturday night and all of Sunday for no extra money. It was either dedication or lunacy, and at the moment he was inclined to think the latter.

CHAPTER FOURTEEN

The Coroner's Court at Offing was a small, cheerless room adjoining the mortuary, but since the inhabitants of the village usually managed to end their lives without incurring the gruesome necessity of an inquest, it was put to only infrequent use and so had never been considered to merit anything better than its bare floor and cold, clammy walls of institutional brown.

The coroner himself, Mr. Kerslake, was a solicitor from a neighbouring town. He was a dry individual who performed his duties with complete adequacy and the same impartiality he showed toward life itself. Police, pathologists, weeping relatives and members of his own profession were all treated with an air of crisp detachment.

Promptly at eleven o'clock on Monday morning, with practically the whole of Offing either packed into his small court or gathered round its approaches, Mr. Kerslake opened his inquest into the death of Susan Andrews.

He gazed with mild scorn at the odd two dozen members of the public who were squeezed uncomfortably into what was grandly known as the public gallery. This consisted of a railed-off space at the back of the court, so confined that even a cocktail hostess would have hesitated to pack in that number. He derived some satisfaction from the thought that they would undoubtedly be cheated of what they had come for, namely a free display of fireworks and drama. Idiots! he thought as he prepared to spread disillusionment through their ranks. In less than ten minutes it'd be all over and they could go and get on with more profitable pursuits if they had any, which he, for one, doubted.

He was on the point of beginning when the door at the back of the court opened and a harassed-looking young man thrust his way through to the front and slid into the otherwise empty row reserved for barristers and solicitors. Unaware of Mr. Kerslake's gaze upon him, the young man proceeded to unfasten his briefcase with one hand and mop his anxious, moist face with the other.

'Who's that?' Manton asked P.C. Newbold, who was standing beside him.

'Never seen him before, sir.'

Meanwhile the young man, who was dressed in impeccable legal garb, eased a finger round the inside of his stiff, white collar, shot his cuffs and sat back.

'Yes?' Mr. Kerslake managed to make the monosyllable sound like the ping of an icicle.

The young man smiled nervously. 'Good morning, sir.'

At this point the coroner's officer, a grizzled constable to whom nothing could come as a surprise, hissed fiercely in the young man's direction, 'Coroner wants to know who you are.'

The young man rose and leaning as far as he could over the desk to bring his head closer to Mr. Kerslake's whispered, 'James Thirkell, sir, of Messrs. Whitehead, Workman and Wench.'

Mr. Kerslake, who had perceptibly shrunk back in his chair as the young man zoomed at him like a roving microphone, now struck back. 'Mr. Treacle, did you say?'

'No, sir, Thirkell. T-H-I-R-K-E-L-L,' the young man replied, blushing furiously.

'And what is your business at this inquest, Mr. Thirkell?' Mr. Kerslake asked with repelling chilliness. He objected to lawyers arriving unheralded in his court, particularly overdressed young ones like Mr. Thirkell. He also happened to have a strong dislike of Mr. Wench, one of the partners in Mr. Thirkell's firm.

Once more Mr. Thirkell leaned as far toward the coroner as safety allowed.

'I hold a watching brief, sir,' he said in an agonised sotto voce.

'On behalf of whom?' Mr. Kerslake asked relentlessly.

Mr. Thirkell, who had been half-way to resuming his seat now swung forward again, a small piece of paper in his outstretched hand.

'My clients' names are written there, sir. I hope you'll agree that it's not necessary to disclose their identity in public . . . not in the interests of anyone connected with the matter . . . certainly fairer not to do so . . . of no real interest . . . could have unfortunate and unfair consequences if . . .'

Mr. Kerslake listened dispassionately to Mr. Thirkell's somewhat inarticulate murmurings until like a piece of tired clockwork they ground to a halt.

'Very well,' he then said in a tone as clear as a mountain spring,' so you hold a watching brief on behalf of Sir James and Lady Neale. Now we can get on.'

Manton and Avis exchanged a quick glance, as Doctor Ryman made his way to the witness-box.

'Just cause of death, doctor,' Mr. Kerslake said laconically.

'Asphyxia.'

The coroner waited with pen poised, but the pathologist remained silent and gazed benignly in Manton's direction.

'What had caused the asphyxia?' Mr. Kerslake was forced to ask at length.

'Oh, so you do want more than the mere cause?' Dr. Ryman remarked indulgently. 'The lass had been strangled by a ligature. The ligature'—he fixed Mr. Kerslake with a triumphant eye—'was her own scarf and she had not died by her own hand.'

'Thank you, we needn't take your evidence further than that today.' The coroner looked toward Mr. Thirkell. 'Any questions?'

'No thank you, sir.'

'I'd like to ask a question.' George Andrews was standing at the end of the row of lawyers' seats and squarely claiming Mr. Kerslake's eye.

'You're the dead girl's father?' Mr. Kerslake asked as a matter of formality.

'Yes.'

'I can't stop you, but do you think it's really necessary? You appreciate these proceedings are largely formal?'

'Yes, but there's one matter I'd like to get on record at the earliest opportunity.'

'Very well.'

Andrews half-turned toward the pathologist. 'Was there any evidence that my daughter had been sexually assaulted either immediately before or after her death?'

'No, there was not.'

'On the other hand, was there evidence to suggest she might have resisted an assault?'

'You mean the button off her blouse?' Dr. Ryman asked amiably.

'Yes.'

'It's certainly one inference to be drawn, that the button had come off in a struggle.'

Andrews nodded his acceptance of the answer

and in a taut voice went on, 'I'd like you to answer this question "yes" or "no". Can you say definitely that my daughter was not a virgin?'

'No, I cannot,' Dr. Ryman replied in a studiously grave tone.

'Thank you. That's all I wish to ask this witness.'

Manton sucked in his lower lip. He couldn't help admiring Andrews's tenacious faith in his daughter's good name, even if, at the same time and for that very reason, he also foresaw endless trouble ahead, for it had already been made clear to him that Andrews was proposing to establish himself as a relentless watchdog over the inquiry.

The next witness was Andrews himself, though his evidence was concerned only with identification of his daughter's body. Mr. Thirkell again had no questions to ask and the coroner dismissed him from the box with a curt nod.

The third and last witness was Manton who gave a short account of the finding of Susan's body, and, in general terms, of the police inquiries which had already been launched. As he was giving his evidence, he noticed Bernard Kingston standing by the door at the back of the court. He hadn't seen him arrive and wondered how long he'd been there. At least *he* hadn't thought it necessary to bring a solicitor along to watch the proceedings.

Mr. Kerslake, who had been writing in his clear, careful hand, now laid down his pen. 'Any questions?' He looked toward Mr. Thirkell who shook his head vigorously and on to Andrews, who nodded.

'Can you say how long it will be before you make an arrest, Superintendent?'

Manton frowned. Of all the bloody silly, inept questions! And coming from an ex-police officer too!

'No, I can't,' he said.

'But you already have a suspect in mind?' Andrews went on, ignoring the chilliness of Manton's tone.

'Is that question either proper or relevant to your present inquiry, sir?' Manton appealed to Mr. Kerslake.

The coroner pursed his lips and made a small fastidious gesture with his hand. 'No, I don't consider it is,' he replied with judicial suavity. 'Any other questions?'

'No.' Andrews stepped back against the wall and stared stonily at the top of Mr. Thirkell's carefully brushed head.

'Then I adjourn this inquest sine die,' Mr. Kerslake announced, and disappeared through the door at the back of the court before the coroner's officer had time to get everyone to their feet.

'Stuff him, anyway!' the officer muttered

disgustedly to himself.

Manton watched Mr. Thirkell close the notebook in which he had never ceased writing since his flurried arrival and decided to see if he could find out anything of interest from the young solicitor. He sidled up to where he had begun re-packing his shiny new briefcase.

'You ran it pretty close,' he said in a friendly tone.

'I know, wasn't it awful!' Mr. Thirkell replied with a grin. 'Matter of fact, it's the first time I've ever been inside a coroner's court. I was scared stiff.'

'You seemed to manage all right.'

'Did I?'

'Well, you didn't have much to do, did you?'

'No, except for that awful bit at the beginning when old Kerslake wanted to know what I was doing here at all.'

'I must say, I wondered too,' Manton's tone was disarming.

'We only received our instructions over the phone this morning. Mr. Wench couldn't come himself, so he despatched me at exactly one minute's notice.'

'Have the Neales been clients of your firm for a long time?'

'Donkeys' years, I believe. But I've been with them only nine months. I was articled to a firm in London before that, but decided I'd prefer practice in the home counties when I was qualified.'

'Do you know Lady Neale?' Manton asked.

'Never set eyes on her,' Mr. Thirkell replied cheerfully.

'I was wondering what her interest was in these proceedings?'

Mr. Thirkell jumped as though Manton had stuck a pin into his behind.

'I say, you're not trying to pump me about our clients' business, are you?'

'Good gracious, no!' Manton exclaimed in mock horror.

'Though, to tell you the truth, I'm not sure either why I was sent along. Mr. Wench didn't tell me, he just said to write down every word that's given in evidence and to keep my ears open for any mention of our clients' name. And then he mentioned about not disclosing our interest in the proceedings.' Mr. Thirkell's expression clouded. 'I'm afraid he's going to be rather annoyed about that, but I don't see what else I could have done. Old Kerslake—well, you heard him—bawled it from the housetops when I passed him that piece of paper with the clients' name on.' He looked at Manton for support.

'Never does to try to hush anything up in court. Only makes the Press smell a rat. Not only the Press either, for that matter. However, if it's of any interest, I'll tell *you* why your clients wanted to be represented. It's because they were worried their son's name might be mentioned in the course of the proceedings.'

'Oh, so you guessed!' Mr. Thirkell said in an abashed tone which caused Manton to wonder who was trying to fool whom. 'Yes, I gather that Lady Neale was afraid someone might try to mention her son's one-time acquaintanceship with the deceased.' He smothered a small snigger. 'Some acquaintanceship! I believe he wanted to throw up Cambridge and run away with the girl. His parents had hell's own difficulty in bringing him back to his senses. They'd even got my firm to oil all the legal machinery in readiness, should the couple suddenly have made a dash for Gretna Green. But that's strictly between ourselves, of course, and anyway it was all many months ago.'

'I didn't realise it'd been as serious as that,' Manton remarked thoughtfully. 'I'm sure *her* parents weren't aware of elopements in the air.'

'Possibly not, but from all I've heard Lady Neale is a forceful sort of mother and Michael a fairly pliant son. I gather the smell of rebellion was short-lived.' He chuckled as he snapped the clasp on his briefcase. 'I must get back to the office, Mr. Wench'll be expecting me.' With a cheerful flip of the hand he gathered up his belongings and fled.

Manton was about to follow him when Sergeant Avis came into court. 'I've just had some news about Kingston, sir.'

134

'He was here a minute ago,' Manton said, looking around the room.

'I saw him leaving as I came along. I told him to go and wait for us at the station,' Avis said. In an excited tone, he went on, 'I've been through to C.R.O., sir, and they've turned up a conviction against him. It appears he was fined for indecent assault on a seventeen-year-old girl twelve years ago. I've made a further check and found that it was at the time his wife was about to give birth to their first daughter.'

'Interesting. Very interesting,' Manton remarked.

'And there's a bit more,' Avis continued. 'I've also discovered that Mrs. Kingston had an operation about six weeks ago as a result of which she's unable to have intercourse.'

'You've had a far more productive morning than I have, Dick,' Manton said, with a wry smile.

'I thought you'd be interested, sir.'

'I am. It's a pity, though, that none of it amounts to evidence.'

Sergeant Avis nodded. 'But it all helps to harden suspicion.'

CHAPTER FIFTEEN

It was a worried-looking Kingston who was waiting when Manton and Avis arrived back at the police station.

'There's something I'd like to get off my chest,' he blurted out as soon as the door of P.C. Newbold's minute office was closed. 'It's about this scratch on my face.' He put a finger up to his cheek. 'I didn't get it from Fred Crowland's kitten, though I admit I asked him to say that I had.'

'Well?'

'I was afraid to tell you the truth when you called in the middle of the night, I didn't want my wife to know what had really happened. You see I'd told her it had been done by old Fred's cat.'

'Go on,' Manton said stonily.

'Well, that's it.'

'It's only half of it. If it wasn't the cat, how did you come by the scratch?'

Out of the corner of his eye Manton saw Avis fish for his notebook. Each of them knew suddenly that the answer to this question could determine the future course of the inquiry.

Contriving to look like a sheepish schoolboy, Kingston said, 'As a matter of fact I got it from one of her ear-rings. It happened when I was giving her a chaste good night kiss. Now you see why I couldn't very well tell my wife.'

'Then we'll doubtless find some of your blood on the ear-ring,' Avis remarked blandly.

Kingston grinned. 'I'm afraid you won't. She was so upset at what had happened, she immediately took it off and wiped it.'

'Was it in the course of this chaste kiss that you also ripped a button off her blouse?' Manton asked.

'No, I never ripped any buttons off anywhere. Look, Superintendent,' his tone became ingratiating, 'I realise I've been a fool. I suppose I oughtn't to have taken her out in the first place and I certainly shouldn't have lied to you when you called in the small hours of yesterday morning, except that you must admit that if anyone has an excuse for being flustered, it's when the police knocks him up at one in the morning. Anyway, that's the truth now and I'm glad to have got it off my chest.'

Manton stirred impatiently in his chair. 'You must take me for a real simpleton if you expect me to believe that lot.' He paused and then said with grating emphasis, 'I wonder if you realise just how close you are to being charged with murder. I not only believe it was you who killed Susan but I'm going to prove it.'

Kingston flinched and ran a nervous finger over his moustache. 'I didn't kill her,' he said hoarsely, 'and I can prove I didn't.'

'How? By more false evidence? Don't forget what happened over Crowland.'

'I can prove that Susan was alive after I left her.' Manton and Avis stared at him suspiciously. 'What's more,' Kingston went on in a rising triumph, 'you know it, too. What about Captain Armstrong's evidence?' He observed Manton's guarded expression. 'You didn't know I knew about him, did you? Luckily, he's had experience of the police before and so wasn't content just to let *you* know what he could testify to. He came along to the court this morning to make sure that what he had to say didn't run any risk of becoming suppressed.'

For a few seconds Manton stared at him with undisguised contempt. Then he said, 'You think you're very clever, don't you, Kingston! But just remember it's the clever ones who generally come unstuck first. Now get out!'

After Avis had taken him out, Manton gazed moodily about the room for a time. He hadn't found it easy to control his feelings at Kingston's jeering tone. And damn Captain Armstrong, too! What had he wanted to go and make a present of that to Kingston at *this* stage! It was obvious that he must be mistaken about having seen Susan just before midnight; it just didn't fit in with the rest of the evidence. And to go and spill it to Kingston just when they had him starting to sweat was the bloody limit!

There'd been a moment at the beginning of the interview when he'd felt himself only one small move away from arresting Kingston, but now they'd have to dig deeper as well as putting what they'd already unearthed back under the microscope. Damn Captain Armstrong!

'I want to have another talk with Christine Thrupp,' he said when Avis returned. 'Let's go now before anyone else thinks of it.'

When they reached the house, the door was opened by Christine herself. She was munching a sandwich and greeted them with surprise. 'Oh . . . hallo!'

'Is your father in?' Manton asked.

'He's at work.'

'Mother?'

'She's out, too.'

'That's splendid, because it's you we wanted to talk to and now we can chat in private.'

The girl looked doubtful. She was dressed in her school uniform, and this gave her a demure appearance that had been wholly absent the first time they'd seen her.

'Dad said not to have anything to do with you if you tried to see me,' she said with a frown.

'As far as we're concerned your Dad needn't know we've called,' Manton said quickly. 'Surely you want to help us find out who killed Susan?'

'All right, then. Come in quick, before anyone sees. If necessary, I'll tell Dad you broke in,' she said in a matter-of-fact tone as she closed the door behind them.

'He'd probably believe it, too,' Avis muttered to Manton, as they followed her along the passage and into the kitchen. Without giving her visitors further attention, she sat down and went on with her lunch while a transistor radio poured out music beside her plate.

Manton pulled a chair out from the table and sat down astride it. Sergeant Avis, after peering about him, elected to go and lean against the sink. Producing from his coat pocket the photograph of Susan and Kingston taken at the Yellow Caravan, Manton pushed it across to Christine.

'Ever seen that man before, Christine?'

She transferred her sandwich to the other hand and temporarily ceased munching as she stared at it with an engrossed expression.

'Who is he?' she asked, in a voice full of curiosity.

'His name's Kingston. Have you ever heard Susan mention him?'

'No.' She shook her head and tilted the photograph as she continued to study it with interest. 'Is that who she was out with on Friday night? How old is he?'

'About thirty-six.'

'Crumbs!'

'Does it surprise you that Susan went out with someone as old as that?'

She hunched up one shoulder. 'She always liked them older; she used to say that boys our age didn't know what to do.' She let out a snigger. 'That they either wanted to neck hard all the time or else you couldn't get them to do anything.' She became thoughtful for a moment. 'But thirty-six!'

'Did Susan ever mention the possibility of eloping with Michael Neale?'

'Running away with him, do you mean?' Her tone was incredulous, and Manton nodded. 'She wasn't that mad on him. Of course, it was nice his having a car and all that, but he used to get her down. She was always saying how he took everything so seriously.'

'Do you know whether they'd seen much of each other recently?'

'I don't think so. It was more or less all over between them. She'd told him she didn't think they were really suited.'

'What was his reaction?'

'He just had to lump it, didn't he? Anyway, he didn't have the ambition to do anything about it, he was a bit drippy like I told you before.'

'This is what Susan herself told you?'

''Course. I've never spoken to him myself.' Then as though she thought this might require further explanation she added, 'Susan always kept her boys to herself. She didn't want any competition.'

Manton received a mental picture of teenage jungle warfare in which even friends were accustomed to cast predatory eyes at one another's conquests. But perhaps it had always been so.

Christine swallowed her last mouthful of sandwich and looked at the clock. 'I'll have to fly in a second. It takes me ten minutes to cycle to school. I don't usually come back middle-day, but I forgot to take my tennis things this morning.'

Manton flicked at a fly which had settled on the edge of the table and was rubbing its front legs together in contemplation of a large crumb. 'Do you happen to know, Christine, whether Susan ever took off her shoes when she was out?' Observing her startled expression, he went on, 'I've known girls do so in the cinema or under the table in a restaurant. I just wondered if Susan did?'

She shook her head. 'She used to refuse to wear her best shoes in Michael's car because she said it spoilt them, but that's all. I've never known her take them off.' She glanced again at the clock. 'Look, I must fly or I'll get into trouble. Miss Summers—she's the games' mistress—is terribly strict.'

'Do you enjoy tennis?' Manton asked idly as he dismounted from the chair.

Christine made an expressive face. 'Depends who's playing. If it's just girls it's dreary, but sometimes the boys are allowed to join in and then it's fun.' She gathered up her belongings. 'I'll go out the front way and you leave by the back. It'll be safer that way.'

Manton doubted the logic of this assertion, but as the front door had already slammed before he could make any reply, he contented himself with a resigned glance at Avis.

Some time very soon it would be necessary to see Christine again and obtain a signed statement of all she had told them. Already the pile of statements was growing as officers fanned out over the countryside like zealous canvassers. Some of the statements would prove to be vital, many would be useless, but the accumulation would continue until the case was over. Manton still had nightmare memories of one unsolved murder investigation which he had led and in which over two thousand statements had been taken, and even this, he knew, was by no means a record.

Sergeant Avis let out a sudden chuckle. 'Bet Thrupp would lay an egg if he knew two policemen had been left alone in his house.'

'Yes, we'd better get out,' Manton said, heading for the back door. As they closed it behind them, he went on, 'Wouldn't you have expected Christine to have been more upset by her friend's death? But she's more interested than grief-stricken.'

Sergeant Avis pursed his lips. 'They're pretty

resilient at that age. They grieve more over the death of a family pet than they do over each other. After all, the majority of school friendships are founded on expediency.'

'That sounds rather cynical, but maybe you're right.'

Making a somewhat circuitous return to their car, they reached it just as a man stepped forward from the shadow of a tree.

'Superintendent Manton, I'm Sankey of the *Morning Herald*. Is it true that an arrest is imminent?'

'Who told you that?'

The newspaperman smiled. 'Somebody whom I thought might know.'

'Then why bother to ask me?'

'You're the bloke in charge, after all. But speaking off the record, you've no doubt Kingston's your man, have you?'

'You know I can't answer that.'

'I did say *off* the record.'

'Even so.'

Sankey smiled again. It was a sardonic, knowing smile, which lacked any warmth. 'Anything the Press can do to help?' he asked, and before Manton could reply, went on, 'Why don't you come over to the King's Head this evening. I'll be there and a number of others as well.' He turned toward Avis. 'Do your best to persuade him, Sergeant.' Then with a casual flip of the hand, he strolled away.

'Cheeky monkey,' Avis growled.

Manton sighed. Unlike some of his colleagues he never felt completely at ease in dealings with the Press. He realised that they could sometimes assist an inquiry; though, in his experience, far less often than they were pleased to boast. On the other hand, if you kept them coldly at arm's length, they were quite capable of dissecting you with exquisite relish when the opportunity arose, which it assuredly would. Somewhere between studied aloofness and bucolic bonhomie, he supposed, lay a happy compromise.

All he knew at the moment, however, was that he had somehow got to reconcile Kingston's statement that he left Susan a few yards from her home at half-past ten with the fact that Captain Armstrong saw her near Langdale Farm two miles away shortly before midnight, and that her dead body was subsequently found in a ditch on Offing Airfield approximately four miles from both these points. The only obvious explanation was that Kingston was lying. He was already a proved liar, so why believe him when he said that he last saw Susan alive at half-past ten. But then if he was lying about that, what was Susan doing walking along a lane two miles from home at midnight? Damn Captain Armstrong! He must be mistaken. But the thing was how to prove it.

As they drove back to the station, Manton

decided to take an early opportunity of returning to London to report to the Assistant Commissioner (Crime). Perhaps the A.C.C. would consider the evidence was strong enough to support a charge against Kingston.

Perhaps! But Manton doubted it.

CHAPTER SIXTEEN

The next morning Manton drove to London and was at the Yard by ten o'clock. He had spent the previous afternoon in a further interview with Captain Armstrong who had, however, remained unshaken in any detail of his story. He was still positive it was Susan he had seen and he was equally positive that it was nearer midnight than half-past eleven that he had seen her.

There had not been time for Manton to avail himself of Sankey's open invitation to join the Press in the King's Head, since after leaving Armstrong he had had to drive over to County Police Headquarters for a conference with the Chief Constable, who, he suspected, wanted to be reassured that he had done the right thing in calling in the Yard. Manton had been able to report activity but little fresh progress in the past twenty-four hours. Indeed, as his car weaved in and out of the morning traffic, he fell to pondering the ironic turn which the investigation had taken. It had got off to a bounding start with one clue leading inexorably to another and then suddenly, just when it seemed certain the whole thing was going to be solved like an easy hand of patience, it had come to a frustrating halt.

When he arrived at the Yard, he made first for the laboratory. He hardly expected them to have got very far, knowing the conditions of chronic congestion under which they permanently worked, and so was agreeably surprised to find that most of the items had already been examined even if it might still be some time before a full report was ready.

However, the information he was given brought him no nearer a quick solution. Susan's nail clippings and scrapings, he was told, had revealed nothing significant and certainly did not include any particles of Kingston's skin or blood.

'In fact, they were surprisingly clean nails,' the scientific officer added.

'Were they short or long?' Manton asked.

'On the long side. I gained the impression that she had well-looked-after hands.'

'Did you find anything on her ear-rings?'

The scientist scanned a page of scrawled notes. 'Ear-rings! Ear-rings!' he murmured. 'Yes, here we are. No, nothing.' He extracted his little finger which had been busily exploring his own left ear, examined the tip and flicked of a lump of wax which missed Manton narrowly. 'I haven't had time yet to complete my tests on all her clothing, but as far as my preliminary examination goes there are no signs of sexual interference. I may find something else, though, which will help you.'

'Dr. Ryman mentioned a piece of cotton which he found caught between her teeth.'

'Yes, I've examined that. There's not much to say about it, except that it is a piece of white cotton.'

'Like a frayed end she had bitten off?'

'Ye-es. It's rather like a thread from a towel, that sort of thing. If you think it's all that important, I'll send it to one of our fabric experts for examination.'

'I don't know whether it'll be important or not, but—'

'I'll have it done anyway. Better to be safe than sorry in a murder case.'

Shortly after this Manton left him burrowing into his other ear and made his way to the floor where the A.C.C. had his room. A couple of minutes' wait in the secretary's office and he was admitted to the A.C.C.'s presence. He was in the act of tying a neat bow on a huge file of papers, and looked up and smiled.

'Hello, Simon.' He usually addressed Manton by his first name when they were alone. 'Sit down and tell me how things are going.'

He listened without interruption while Manton talked, occasionally stretching forward to straighten an object on his desk or to make a quick note on a small creamy pad at his side.

'It's this fellow Armstrong, sir, who's thrown a fistful of sand in the works. Moreover, he's one of those witnesses who will become more determined he's right with every suggestion that he may have made a mistake.'

'Has it occurred to you,' the A.C.C. asked, after staring pensively for some time at his silver inkstand, 'that Armstrong could be right and Kingston could still have murdered the girl?' He switched his gaze abruptly to Manton. 'Mightn't the sequence of events have been as follows? Kingston drops the girl somewhere around half-past ten, probably a fair distance from her home, he spends an hour or so with this fellow Crowland and then after that he picks Susan up again, by which time she's been seen by Armstrong?'

'But why should he have done that, sir?' Manton asked in a bewildered tone.

'I don't know . . . but wait a moment.' He suddenly held up an admonitory finger. 'Supposing he had refused to drive Susan back to Offing because she wasn't willing to neck with him, and had just dumped her and told her she could walk, don't you think in those circumstances he might have had second thoughts and gone back to look for her,

149

particularly as he was still in the area an hour or so later?'

'That's a clever theory, sir,' Manton said admiringly.

'Yes, but theory is all it is. One could hardly invite a court to consider it unless it was supported by evidence.' He shifted in his chair. 'But the thing that strikes me about the case, Simon, is the intrusive presence of this young fellow, Neale. I can't help thinking you ought to concentrate your efforts on clearing him out of the way, assuming of course your inquiries don't have the opposite effect. At the moment he's far too obvious a red herring for Kingston's advisers to miss. He knew the dead girl, he was in Offing the day she was murdered and indeed, although he told you he spent that Friday evening in London, someone—albeit someone with a motive—has come forward to say he saw him driving about the village in the course of the evening.' The A.C.C. picked up a paper-knife and jabbed the air with it. 'Once you can eliminate Neale, you'll have Kingston in much stronger focus. Anyway, that's the line along which I'd tackle it if I was in charge of the inquiry. Sooner or later we shall probably have to draw up a balance sheet of evidence for and against Kingston and fix up a conference with the Director to get his opinion. In the meantime, however, we'll hope you can scratch up a bit more against him.' With quiet emphasis he went on, 'No need to impress on you what an important inquiry this is. The public always gets more steamed up over cases involving children, not unnaturally, while the Press, of course, churn out all the harrowing details, not wholly blind to increasing their sales.'

After leaving the A.C.C. Manton poked his head round a few doors to exchange greetings with some of his colleagues, but by noon he was on his way back to Offing. Before setting out on his return journey, he had spoken to Sergeant Avis on the telephone. It appeared, however, that nothing fresh had developed in the three hours he had been away. Nothing, that is, save the somewhat ominous piece of news that Andrews had been seen holding a press conference at his front gate.

All in all, he returned to Offing with a singular lack of relish.

CHAPTER SEVENTEEN

One hour after arriving back in Offing, Manton was off again, this time accompanied by Sergeant Avis and with Cambridge as their destination. A telephone call had been put through to Michael Neale who had suggested a certain road-house on the road in from London as providing a suitable rendezvous. This proved to be another mock-Tudor one-storey establishment squatting in a vast asphalt acreage which was empty apart from Neale's own red sports car.

They found him sitting at a table in the equally empty lounge and morosely turning the pages of an old *Illustrated London News*. A middle-aged female wearing a flowered smock approached as the officers joined Neale. Her voice was as pseudo as the building.

'Three set teas?'

'No, just three cups of tea, please,' Manton replied.

'You'll have to have a pot for three,' she said acidly. 'We don't serve cups of tea.'

While they were waiting for the tea to come, Manton remarked, 'You couldn't have chosen anywhere quieter to meet, that's for certain.'

Neale gave an abstracted nod. He was dressed in a pair of fawn trousers and a sports jacket with leather-patched elbows, and Manton was again struck by his heavily-lidded eyes, which gave him the appearance of having difficulty in keeping awake.

The female returned with the tea which she deposited disdainfully on the table and took herself off once more to the kitchen. Manton then opened the proceedings. 'When I saw you two days ago, Mr. Neale, you told me you had spent Friday evening up in London.'

'Yes, that's right.'

'I'd like to know the names of anyone you were with.'

Neale moistened his lips. 'I was at a friend's party in Chelsea. His name's Robert Sheldon and he has a flat in Beaufort Street.'

'How many people were there at this party?'

'At least forty or fifty.'

'And you went to it alone?'

'Yes.'

'And left alone?'

'Yes.'

'Can you give me the names of any of the people you talked to while you were there?'

Neale shook his head slowly. ''Fraid not. It wasn't the sort of party where people were introduced, and apart from Rob himself I didn't know anyone.'

'Surely you must have heard some of their names; you must have picked up one or two.'

Neale appeared to be racking his brain. In a tentative voice he said, 'I talked to a girl called Tania and another called Rosie, at least I think her name was Rosie: also to a chap whom everyone referred to as Mac.' He frowned hard at the teapot. 'I think those are the only names I can recall.'

Sergeant Avis turned over the page of his notebook and waited.

'What time did you arrive at the party?' Manton asked.

'About eight o'clock.'

'And leave?'

'I can't remember.'

'Try to remember.'

'What's the use, it'd only be a guess!'

'Guess then.'

'It's stupid.'

'What time did you arrive home?'

Neale ran a finger round the rim of his saucer. 'About two o'clock, I believe.'

'Did you drive straight home?'

'Yes.'

'Then presumably you must have left Chelsea around one o'clock?'

'I suppose so,' he said dully.

'What's your answer if I tell you that someone says they saw you in Offing between half-past ten and eleven that night?'

'Who says that?'

'Never mind who, what's your answer?'

'That they must be mistaken. Mine isn't the only red sports car in the village, you know.'

'Are you quite certain that you never saw Susan Andrews that evening?'

Neale slowly lifted his eyes to meet Manton's. 'Quite certain,' he said in a steady voice.

'Why did you come home last week-end?'

'To go to Rob Sheldon's party.'

'Wouldn't it have been more usual to have driven straight to London from here?'

'Possibly, but I was able to get away in the

early afternoon and decided to call in and see my parents. In fact, they weren't at home since they were not expecting me. I had only told my mother that I would be home to sleep.'

In the silence which followed Avis cupped his mouth and whispered to Manton who gave a nod. A second later Avis got up and left the room. Manton leant forward to resume his cross-examination. The pallor of Neale's cheeks seemed to have increased, but otherwise he appeared to be quite in control of himself.

'Is it true that Susan Andrews had grown a little tired of your attentions?' he asked in a brutal tone.

Neale bit his lip, and when he looked up, Manton saw that his eyes were filled with tears.

'No, *I* don't think so. You have to remember she was only sixteen. At that age, one's emotions are more fluid.' He caught Manton's expression. 'Oh, I know I'm only six years older, but that makes a big difference. I'm quite sure in my heart that Susan loved me as much as I loved her.'

'Hadn't she told you that she didn't consider you properly suited to one another?'

There was a momentary flash of anger in Neale's eyes, like an unheralded flicker of summer lightning.

'That's what I'm trying to explain,' he said. 'She sometimes said things she didn't mean. Anyway,' he added, 'she never said that.'

'Were you hoping to marry her one day?'

'Yes.'

'Even against your parents' wishes?'

'If necessary.'

'And you can offer no suggestion as to who killed her?'

'None, none, none,' he cried, thumping the table with his fist. 'Isn't it bad enough to lose the one person in the world you adored more than any other without all these questions?' For a minute or two he looked about him with a wild expression, then in a strained voice he said, 'I'm sorry about that outburst.'

'Did you ever hear Susan mention the name of Bernard Kingston?' Manton asked, as though nothing had happened.

'I'm sorry . . . I wasn't listening properly . . . what name?'

'Kingston. Bernard Kingston?'

'No.' He shook his head.

A few minutes later Avis returned and Manton sent him off to find the flowered female and pay the bill. Outside a brief farewell was exchanged before they drove away in their opposite directions.

'Well?' Manton asked, when he and Avis were in the car.

'I managed to speak to Sheldon, sir. He confirms that Neale came to his party last Friday evening, but hasn't the faintest idea what time he left. I gather it was one of those parties where nobody remembers very much at all afterwards. There appears to have been people coming and going all the time between eight and four the next morning. Sounded a bit like a main-line station in the rush hour.'

Manton pursed his lips. 'Nevertheless, I think we'd better send someone along to see Sheldon and obtain a complete list of his guests, both invited and uninvited—or at any rate as many as he's able to remember.'

'You're not happy about Neale, sir?' Avis asked.

'I don't know what to think about him,' Manton replied with a heavy sigh. 'All I am sure of is that he's a complicated young man.'

CHAPTER EIGHTEEN

Susan's funeral was held on Wednesday morning, the coroner having issued his certificate that the burial could take place. The church was packed for the occasion and every organisation in the village was represented.

Manton, Avis and two officers of the county force attended and occupied a pew at the back from which they could keep an observant eye on the whole proceeding, not that they expected to learn very much. Ahead of them was a phalanx of staff and pupils from Susan's school, amongst whom Manton recognised Christine. She turned her head constantly to view the comings and goings, and from time to time whispered to the girls on either side of her. In the front pew Manton could see George Andrews sitting like a figure of stone, while his wife leaned against him, giving the impression that she would topple over but for his presence. Beyond them, in the chancel, Susan's coffin rested across two wooden trestles.

The service began and Manton tried to compose his mind with thoughts appropriate to the occasion, but after a while gave up in rueful despair and allowed it to roam where it would. The trouble was that to mourn, other than in a general way, for someone you had never met required a greater sense of Christian piety than he could muster. He found it equally difficult to feel more than limited sympathy for someone like George Andrews who, he knew, regarded *him* with thinly veiled hostility.

The vicar, an earnest man with a tremulous lower lip and an emotional ring to his voice, announced a hymn.

'Tender Shepherd, thou has still'd
Now thy little lamb's brief weeping . . .'

sang the congregation with uncertain fervour, and Manton was surprised to discover that Avis possessed an attractive tenor voice and obviously enjoyed using it.

The priest's address followed. Manton listened with morbid fascination as one emotionally charged cliché followed another. He would have liked to be moved by what he heard, but instead found himself recoiling from the flow of platitudinous sentiment. It occurred to him not for the first time that death created the one human situation which few were equipped to deal with naturally. All too often it seemed to induce a mixture of embarrassment and contrived emotion, surely distasteful alike to God and his servant sufferer.

The service came to an end and Susan's coffin was borne slowly down the aisle. All around, women were weeping and men gazed misty-eyed at the short, solemn procession. There was a slight hold-up as the coffin came level with Manton and he was able to see the inscription on the only wreath resting on it. It read:

'In memory of our darling daughter from her ever adoring mother and father.'

The procession jerked on, and a little later the officers themselves emerged into the warm sunshine of a May morning.

'I didn't see either Kingston or Neale there,' Avis remarked as they walked over to their car.

'I hardly expected to,' Manton replied

gloomily. 'I suppose we had better go to the cemetery now.'

Offing cemetery lay on the outskirts of the village, and by the time they arrived the service of commitment had begun. They stood on the fringe of the crowd where they were able to move about discreetly. In the open air there wasn't the same oppressive atmosphere that had prevailed in church. A sardonic voice suddenly came floating over Manton's shoulder.

'I see that the police are mingling with the graveside mourners.' Manton turned to find Sankey just behind him. The newspaperman gave him a small, twisted smile and went on, 'A time-honoured practice, isn't it? Not that I see your chief suspect amongst those present.'

'And what's the Press hoping to pick up here?'

'Tch! tch! No need to sound so edgy, Superintendent. We have a job to do the same as you, except that we don't always receive as much help as we give.'

Manton was about to turn away when Sankey continued, 'Have you spoken to George Andrews today?'

'No. Why?'

'Oh, I just wondered. I think he'd like to have a word with you sometime.'

Manton looked at him suspiciously and was met with an innocent smile. 'Are you up to something?' he asked grimly.

'Oh, for heaven's sake, Superintendent! I ask you a perfectly innocent question which you answer, and then you begin to act like M.I.5 and 6 rolled into one. Anyway, don't forget, I've told you something; next time it'll be your turn.'

He strolled off, casting his gaze over the mourners rather like a racegoer picking his horse for the next race.

'I don't like the way things are going, Dick,' Manton said. 'If George Andrews allows himself to be ensnared by the Press, we're in for a sticky time.'

Ten minutes later the mourners, watched by Avis, were departing while Manton made his way to the graveside to look at the wreaths. There were upwards of two dozen, mostly of spring flowers, though a few of more traditional laurel and evergreen. There was one from the staff of the school, another from the girls of Susan's form. Yander's had also sent their tribute, but the largest wreath of all was from the Press.

A small bunch of wild flowers caught Manton's eye, and he bent down to look at the card which read:

'Susan, from M.N.'

Neale had presumably not dared to express himself more openly, but there was something touching about the tiny bunch of flowers with its simple card.

'Always interesting seeing who's sent what, isn't it?' Manton didn't need to turn round to know that Sankey had joined him.

'Indeed,' he replied blandly, determined not to be thrown on the defensive again. 'I was just admiring that very large one over there.'

Sankey smirked. 'We had a whip round last night.'

'After the bar had closed?'

Somewhat to Manton's surprise, Sankey threw back his head and laughed. 'All right, I know! I always say there aren't two more disillusioned bodies of men than the police and the Press. And yet curiously enough—and you and I both know this is true—there's more genuine camaraderie in our two outfits than you'll find anywhere else.' Manton, who had always held that a crime reporter would shop his own grandmother for a good story, decided, however, to remain silent on this occasion.

In a casual tone, Sankey went on, 'Have you got any forwarder since our chat the day before yesterday?'

'Possibly.'

'Did you know that George Andrews had been making a few inquiries on his own?'

'Is that what he wants to see me about?'

Sankey nodded, but Manton felt that it wasn't in answer to his question. 'I expect that's it.'

Well, if Sankey hoped he was going to be pumped, he was to be disappointed, since Manton had no intention of giving him that satisfaction.

Manton stared over the now deserted cemetery. 'Be seeing you,' he said, and walked off in the direction of the gate where Avis was patiently waiting for him.

Not long after their return to the station Manton was called to the telephone. 'Mr. Andrews would like to speak to you, sir,' P.C. Newbold said.

Now he would most likely learn what was behind Sankey's remarks. He took the receiver and heard muffled voices the other end of the line. It was clear only that they were male voices. Manton just had time to wonder, and guess, who was with Andrews when the latter spoke.

'I'd like to ask you a question, Superintendent.'

'Go ahead.'

'Have you made up your mind to charge anyone yet?'

'No.'

'I see.' The tone was stiffly reproving. 'Do you expect to be in a position to make an arrest within, say, the next twenty-four hours?'

'I'm afraid I'm unable to answer that question.'

'I see,' Andrews said again. Then: 'I think I ought to tell you that I'm not satisfied and that if you've not made an arrest by tomorrow evening, I shall take my own action.'

'What action do you propose taking, Mr. Andrews?' Manton asked, with a frown.

'I shall apply to the magistrates myself for a warrant against a named person.' He paused. 'It's probably better I shouldn't mention the name over the telephone.'

Manton felt like someone who'd been told that the fuse was about to be lit which would blow up Scotland Yard. 'I'd like to have a chat with you,' he said, trying to put a humouring note into his voice. 'May I come and see you?'

'I'll be in for the rest of the day.'

'Fine, I'll be along within the hour.' He replaced the receiver and took a deep breath which he slowly expelled.

So that was it. Andrews was trying to force their hand and if the *police* didn't arrest Kingston, he was going to take steps to institute a private prosecution. As an ex-police officer he was of course well aware of the ins and outs of the law.

Too well aware for Manton's liking.

*   *   *

Manton had half-expected to find Sankey lurking behind a piece of furniture in

Andrews's cottage, but so far as he could see the newspaperman was nowhere about. Andrews, he observed, was still dressed in the dark suit he had worn at the funeral, and his black knitted tie had all the appearance of a symbol of reproach.

'My wife's resting,' he said, as they sat down. 'The funeral was too much of a strain for her. I tried to dissuade her from coming to the cemetery but she insisted on subjecting herself to the ordeal.'

Manton made a sympathetic face. He was finding the atmosphere in the small, melancholy room oppressive after the sunlight outside, but pulled himself together when he realised that Andrews was keeping him under steady gaze and obviously waiting for him to speak. When he did so, his tone reflected both his anxiety and a sense of understanding.

'I know you're impatient to have the fellow who murdered your daughter brought to account, but it's not going to help if you start applying for warrants before the police have had the chance of completing their inquiries. The time for that, if at all, will surely be when we're forced to admit failure and the inquiry has completely run down. At the moment that's far from being the case and I, for one, refuse to acknowledge that there's any smell of failure in the air.'

'But the fact remains,' Andrews said in a

voice which, though quiet, did nothing to conceal the toughness of his mood, 'that you don't consider you have sufficient evidence against Kingston to justify his arrest.'

'True. But I'm confident we shall get enough in the end.'

'And when do you think that'll be?'

'How do I know! All I can promise you is that it won't be a minute later than I can make it.'

'I'm afraid that's not good enough for me.'

A note of exasperation came into Manton's voice. 'But what do you think you're going to gain by striking off on your own? You know as well as I do that the magistrates won't grant you a warrant against Kingston so long as they're informed that police inquiries are still continuing.'

Andrews shrugged. 'It'll focus attention on the case.'

'Ginger us up, you mean!' Manton remarked bitterly. 'And what more attention do you want focused on the case? Every newspaper in the land is already covering the investigation. All you *will* succeed in achieving is making it more difficult for the police to do their job properly.'

'I'm sorry, but that's not the way I see it. I *think* there is enough evidence to justify your arresting Kingston, and if you won't act then I will.' He brushed aside Manton's protest. 'I agree that the magistrates probably won't issue a warrant on my application—you'll be able to see to that—but if they won't and if you still don't make an arrest, then I'll have another full-blooded crack at Kingston when the inquest is resumed.' His tone was diamond-hard. 'I know it's all very unconventional, Superintendent, but it just happens to be your bad luck that I'm an ex-police officer and know all the ropes.'

'I should have thought,' Manton remarked ruefully, 'that, as an ex-police officer, you'd have shown a better appreciation of our difficulties.'

Andrews brusquely shook his head. 'That line cuts no ice with me, I'm afraid. I'm just a father whose innocent daughter has been brutally murdered. I want to see justice done and quickly.' He paused. 'I'm sorry we don't see eye to eye, but that's all there is to that.'

Manton shifted in his chair. 'But this is bloody ridiculous!' he exclaimed. 'Each of us has the same objective at heart and yet you're deliberately going to complicate my job. Can't you at least wait until we've completed our inquiries?'

'Time is against you; you know that as well as I do. Every day that passes without your making an arrest decreases the chance that you ever will.'

'You realise,' Manton asked, in a voice of weary resignation, 'that you'll be required, as a private applicant, to tender evidence in support of your application?'

'Naturally.'

'Since I shall certainly be asked the question by my superiors, may I inquire whether you have any evidence up your sleeve which I don't know about?' Andrews appeared to hesitate and Manton added, 'I'm told that you've been making a few inquiries on your own.'

'Oh?'

'Isn't it true, then?'

Andrews frowned. 'If you must know, what happened was that one of the newspaper fellows gave me a piece of information which I later checked and found to be correct. It was that Kingston didn't reach his home until half-past one in the morning after he had taken out Susan. A neighbour heard him putting away his car.'

'That all?'

'At present, yes,' Andrews replied, in a tone which clearly implied that further private inquiry was not to be ruled out.

Manton rose and stared out of the window at the sun-dappled field across the lane. Two milk-chocolate cows were quietly chewing the cud, and he found himself filled with sudden envy of their placid life. He turned back into the room. 'I can only hope that you'll have second thoughts about this and decide not to take any premature action.'

Andrews's tone, when he replied, was that of a man whose mind is irrevocably made up.

'And I hope you'll decide to save me the necessity.'

CHAPTER NINETEEN

Eight men sat round a table in a first-floor room in Buckingham Gate. In front of each was an expanse of green blotting paper, a small notepad and a newly-sharpened pencil. The scene was the conference room in the Department of the Director of Public Prosecutions. The Director himself presided, flanked by two senior members of his staff. On either side of them, facing each other across the table, sat the A.C.C., Manton and Avis representing the Yard, and the Chief Constable and Detective-Inspector from the county force.

Manton gazed at the pale-green wall opposite him where three framed photographs of previous Directors hung. Around him there was a general confabulation going on. The Director raised his voice at the end of the table.

'Well, gentlemen, shall we begin? What we have to decide is the action to be taken in the light of Andrews's threat to apply for a warrant. We all know the present position with regard to the inquiry and I think we're in general agreement that we haven't enough evidence at this stage to justify Kingston's arrest.' He looked round the table as though for confirmation of this view and received a mixture of nods and expectant expressions. 'On the other hand there is absolutely nothing we can do to prevent Andrews taking this action, persuasion as I understand it having failed, and the only question is whether we should, so to speak, jump the gun; that is, arrest Kingston before we have all our tackle in order, or sit back and do nothing. By that I don't mean literally do nothing, but, simply, continue the inquiry as though nothing was happening.' His glance again went round the seven faces which were turned toward him. 'Personally, I have no doubt myself which is the proper course.' He paused. 'Namely, continue as though Andrews didn't exist.'

The Chief Constable cleared his throat. 'I was hoping, Director, that you might consider there was just sufficient evidence to justify Kingston being charged.'

'I agree he's got a lot to answer,' the Director said quickly. 'But we have to remember that our job is to muster a prima facie case against him. At the present moment the evidence is full of holes, and we can't arrest him in the hope he'll make good the deficiencies himself later.'

The Chief Constable, who had been drawing the hind view of an elephant on his pad, gave it a final embellishment and said, 'And what happens if the magistrates do issue a warrant? We're going to look pretty silly, aren't we?'

'You don't seriously believe they will, do you?' the Director asked in a startled tone.

'Magistrates are like juries; there's no knowing what they'll do.'

For a few seconds, the Director stared thoughtfully down the table while the rest awaited his deliberation on this discordant note. On reflection Manton realised that he wasn't very surprised at the Chief Constable's reluctance to accept police inaction. He was clearly the one who was most exposed to external pressures, not least of which was the circumstance of the dead girl being the daughter of his former detective-inspector.

'Well,' the Director said with slow emphasis, 'I shall still be most surprised if they do grant Andrews's application. But if they do, then of course under the regulations I have to take over the conduct of the ensuing proceedings. And that will presumably mean that we shall present all the available evidence and see whether or not the magistrates consider it sufficient for a committal for trial. And if it's no stronger than it is at this moment, I don't see that they can properly commit him. You'll recall that in the Arundel case, the magistrates issued a warrant for murder on a private application but subsequently dismissed the charge when all the evidence had been led. Also, in that case, of course, the police investigation had more or less reached a full stop.' He paused and lit a cigarette. 'I confess I'm taken aback by Andrews's display of intransigence. It's hardly what one would expect from an ex-detective-inspector.'

The Chief Constable blew out his cheeks. 'You've not met him! Though he was a good officer, he was never an easy person to get along with. His biggest handicap has been a neurotic wife, but he was always inclined to carry a chip on his shoulder.' He gave a helpless shrug. 'As you probably gather, I very much wish the present impasse could have been avoided. I naturally accept your decision, Director, that we mustn't yet arrest Kingston, but I can't hide my concern at all the damaging publicity that's bound to accompany Andrews's action, not to mention the inference that my men have fallen down on the job.'

'It's surely my man who's going to carry any cans back,' the A.C.C. observed quietly, indicating Manton with a gesture of his head.

'The publicity we probably can't avoid,' the Director broke in, 'but I'm sure no one's going to suggest that the police have been guilty of failure just because Andrews makes a private application for a warrant.'

'I hope you're right,' the Chief Constable said gloomily, 'but I'm still going to get my tin hat out of the cupboard when I return to headquarters.'

'Well, that's settled then,' the Director said with a wry smile, pushing back his chair. 'In the meantime, let's wish Mr. Manton luck.' He turned to the Yard officer. 'Isn't it possible that the laboratory will come through with something?'

'They haven't as yet, sir,' Manton replied. 'Nothing of evidential value was found in Kingston's car and I'm not very hopeful that the girl's clothing will provide any clues.'

'What about the piece of cotton caught between her teeth?'

'I'm waiting for a further report about that.'

The Chief Constable pulled out his pipe and blew through it noisily. 'I suppose the clerk to the magistrates had better be warned what's going to happen?'

The Director nodded. 'Yes, I agree. Perhaps you could see him, Mr. Manton. Just tell him that Andrews may make this application but that your inquiries are still continuing. No need to say more than that; we don't want suggestions made later that we tried to nobble the magistrates in advance.'

'Supposing, sir, he wants me to be around when Andrews makes his application?' Manton asked.

'Then be around, but make sure everyone knows you're there at the court's request.'

The conference broke up, and just over an hour later Manton and Avis were back in Offing.

'Good grief, what on earth's going on?' Manton exclaimed as their car rounded the last bend before the police station, for the whole road was blocked with vans and television equipment, and there being interviewed with the station as a background was George Andrews.

Turning to Avis as he prepared to fight his way through the cameras and looped cables which festooned the entrance, Manton said grimly, 'If all this lot isn't cleared away within a quarter of an hour, you can beat Andrews to his application. You can go to court and get a sheaf of summonses for obstruction.'

CHAPTER TWENTY

It was late afternoon before Manton was able to give his attention to the further pile of statements which had gathered on the desk in P.C. Newbold's appropriated office. The road outside the police station had now been cleared and Manton had officially informed Andrews of the decision reached in conference with the Director that morning. He had also spoken to Mr. Ellis, the magistrates' clerk, who had sounded surprisingly unmoved by the prospect of Andrews's application. Manton mentioned this to Newbold.

'Nothing upsets Mr. Ellis,' the local constable replied. 'He's got a big private income, you see.'

'What has that to do with his unflappability?'

'Well, money gives you independence, doesn't it? It enables you to speak your mind and do as you like without worrying what somebody'll think.' He rubbed his chin. 'Our magistrates could be a proper handful without a clerk like Mr. Ellis to guide them.'

'How do you think he'll advise them on Andrews's application?' Manton asked with sudden interest.

'I'm not making any guesses about that! All I'm saying is that it won't throw him into a panic just because it's unusual.'

Feeling that their conversation had taken a certain Alice-in-Wonderland turn, Manton decided not to pursue it further, but to direct his mind to the bunch of statements in front of him. As he read his way through them, it seemed that no one in Offing had escaped interview. Alas, however, it was soon equally apparent that none of the statements took the case further. Discounting the few who raised outrageously wild hares, the great majority of those interviewed had not seen either Susan or Kingston on the evening in question, nor did any of them have any recollection of observing Neale's car, so that Caunt's statement remained uncorroborated. This, on further reflection, Manton decided, might be of more positive value. It seemed to indicate that Caunt must have come forward out of pure malice.

But what was particularly noticeable about the statements—most of them by people who had known Susan personally—was the variety of opinions expressed, in passing, about her. She was variously described as being 'a nicely-spoken, well-mannered girl' to 'boy-crazy' and 'a bit on the precocious side'. This last came from the art master at her school, who, Manton noted, was thirty years old and a bachelor.

It was abundantly clear that not everyone shared her parents' opinion of her, and that she had been successful in concealing from them those facets of her character which she must have known would incur their disapproval, if not something stronger. She had possessed, it seemed, the dubious talent of being able to project her personality in different guises to different people. The quiet, home-loving girl was also the youthful deceiver who was not unversed in cynical opportunism.

P.C. Newbold poked his head round the door and hissed, 'Mr. Kingston's here, sir. He'd like to speak to you urgently.'

Manton raised his eyebrows. 'What's this, a

confession coming up? O.K., show him in.'

A minute later Kingston was ushered into the tiny office, scowling furiously, and his heavy black moustache bristling with outrage. It was as though a threatening black cloud had settled outside the window.

'What's all this about Andrews obtaining a warrant for my arrest?' he burst out.

'Where did you hear that?'

'Somebody at Yander's told me.'

'As far as I know it isn't true, yet.'

'What do you mean by *yet*?'

'That Andrews hasn't yet made an application to the magistrates.'

'What the flaming hell has Andrews got to do with it? What right has he to try and get me arrested?'

'The same right as anyone else,' Manton replied, not without quiet satisfaction at Kingston's perturbation.

'What the hell are you talking about? If Andrews tries anything funny, I'll sue him in every court in the land.'

'If you calm down a minute, I'll endeavour to explain the position to you.'

When Manton had finished speaking, Kingston said in a shaken voice, 'Do you mean to say that I could be arrested and charged with murder as a result of this lunatic's action?'

'If the magistrates grant his application, yes.'

'But it's . . . it's . . . it's monstrous, it's

177

outrageous! I thought the police were the only people who could arrest a person.'

'When I decide to arrest you,' Manton said in a steely voice, 'I shall do so without a warrant. But if anyone else wants to see you charged, they must first obtain a warrant.'

Kingston shook his head in disbelief and put up a hand to wipe away the beads of perspiration which had broken out over his brow. 'Do you mean to say that any madman could apply for my arrest?'

'Yes, but not necessarily with success,' Manton replied with sardonic enjoyment.

Kingston grunted. 'Well, if that's the law, the sooner it's altered the better, otherwise we're all liable to be arrested at the whim of a bloody lunatic.'

'Hardly.'

'Anyway, I shall fight the application tooth and nail. I'll hire the best lawyer money can obtain.'

'You can't.'

'Can't what?'

'Oppose the application. It's what's called ex parte, which means that no one has any right to be there apart from Andrews himself.'

Kingston suddenly sagged, deflated as a wind-sock in a summer breeze. 'You'll do what you can to help me, won't you?'

A dreamy expression came over Manton's face. 'I might be ready to help you; that is, if

178

you were to help me—by admitting you killed Susan Andrews.'

Kingston recoiled as though he had been struck by a cobra. 'But I didn't kill her,' he said vehemently. 'And you have no evidence that I did.'

'I wouldn't say *none*; just not enough at the moment.' His tone changed abruptly and became hard. 'But all the same everything points to you; you were the last person to be seen with her and you've lied to the police.'

Kingston swallowed nervously. 'You're just trying to scare me into confessing something I'm not guilty of.'

'Why don't you tell me the truth?' Manton said impatiently.

'I have.'

'You found her a provocative little piece, didn't you?' His voice was harsh and full of contempt.

'No.'

'That's why you dated her, wasn't it? You thought she'd be a nice easy tumble.'

'That's absurd.'

'After all, it wouldn't be the first time you've made a pass at a young girl, would it?' Kingston stared at him stupidly. 'You've not forgotten, have you, your conviction for indecently assaulting a seventeen-year-old girl twelve years ago?'

'That was different . . . it was . . . well, if I'd

been properly defended I'd have got off. It was a miscarriage of justice.'

'Yeah, it always is!' Manton remarked caustically. 'Your wife had a recent operation, didn't she?'

'Yes, but what's that got to do with your investigation?'

'Possibly quite a lot. You've not been able to have intercourse with her since then, have you?'

Kingston stared at him with disbelieving eyes. 'You're a devil! Fancy raking over my private life like that.' Manton waved aside the protest with a gesture of impatience. 'I'm investigating a murder, not playing a gentlemanly game of cricket. Why don't you admit you strangled Susan?'

'Because I *didn't*.'

'Have you always been over-sexed?'

'No . . . I mean I'm not saying I am.'

'No? Why did you invite Susan out that evening?'

'I've explained that to you before. It was something which happened on the spur of the moment.'

Manton shook his head. 'Not likely. I happen to know that Susan went to special trouble to doll herself up for that evening out with you. That was a well-planned outing, so don't try to kid me otherwise.' He looked up sharply. 'What prompted your invitation?'

'I'd met her a couple of times or so at

company functions, she seemed a pleasant girl, so I didn't see why I shouldn't ask her out.'

'With a view to seducing her?'

'Certainly not.'

'Why then?'

'I tell you, because I liked her.'

'Are you happily married?'

'Of course.'

'Then what were you wanting to take out sixteen-year-old schoolgirls for?'

Kingston ran a finger across his brow and wiped it on his trouser leg. 'Can't a man have an innocent evening out with a girl?'

'No, not when he's married and your age and the girl is only sixteen. You were hoping to seduce her before the evening was out, weren't you? Go on, admit it.'

Kingston squirmed in his chair. 'I don't know what I was hoping for. One doesn't plan these things ahead.'

'No?' Kingston flushed beneath his swarthiness and Manton went on, 'You were angry with her, were you not, when she made it plain she didn't care for you in your rôle of Don Juan?'

'Of course not.'

'Were you pleased, then?'

'I was neither angry nor pleased. I was indifferent.'

'Indifferent? After all the trouble you'd taken to plan the evening? No one's going to believe that. The truth is you strangled her because she wouldn't give in to you, isn't it?'

'She was seen alive after I'd left her,' Kingston retorted defiantly.

'Ah, but I have a theory about that too. I believe that when you left Crowland, you picked her up again, and it was then that you murdered her.'

'How could I have picked her up again?' Kingston asked in a tone which was suddenly wary. 'I'd dropped her just near her home.'

'On the contrary, you dropped her way out in the country, somewhere between the Yellow Caravan and Langdale Farm, where Captain Armstrong saw her. That's right, isn't it?'

For answer Kingston ran two fingers round the inside of his collar and stretched his neck with a tortured grimace.

'Why don't you admit you killed her?' Manton urged again. 'You'll make it easier for everyone if you do.'

'You'll never get me to admit it, not even if you keep me here all night.'

'No one's keeping you here at all. It was you who came knocking on my door, if you remember. Nevertheless, don't be too sure that the time won't come when you'll be glad to make a complete confession.'

Without giving Kingston any opportunity of calling this piece of bluff, Manton rose and opened the door. Soon after Kingston had left,

Avis came into the office.

'He looked a bit shaken up, sir,' he remarked.

Manton nodded slowly. 'Mmm, I even thought he might break at one moment, but either I'm losing my touch or he really didn't do it.'

CHAPTER TWENTY-ONE

Although he had heard nothing official about Andrews's application, Manton decided that he had better not stir too far from base the next morning. And this proved as well, since shortly before half-past ten he received a laconic message from Mr. Ellis asking him to attend court immediately.

Offing Magistrates' Court was at the opposite end of the village to the police station, and was a small vaulted building in Victorian grey stone and with frosted windows. When Manton arrived there, he found a throng of people around the entrance, including the now ubiquitous television camera. Sankey stepped forward as he got out of the car.

'Andrews is in with the magistrates now,' he said with his warily ingratiating smile. 'Have you come along to spike his guns?'

Remembering the Director's admonition,

Manton shook his head. 'I've come only because the court has asked me to.'

'What do you imagine they'll want from you?'

'I've no idea. Perhaps nothing.'

'You've heard that they're taking his application in private, but are proposing to announce their decision in open court?'

'No, I didn't know that, but it sounds a sensible course.' With a faint glint in his eye, he went on, 'You seem to know most things—tell me how many magistrates are sitting?'

'Four. Three men—and Lady Neale.'

Manton was aware of Sankey's gaze on him at the mention of the last name. The reporter clearly hoped for an interesting flicker of reaction, but Manton accepted the information with a mere nod.

'What do you think Andrews's chances are?' Sankey went on after a pause. 'Personally, I don't believe he has a hope in hell.'

'I wouldn't know,' Manton replied in a strictly neutral tone, and turned to enter the building. The uniformed court inspector came across to him. 'Mr. Ellis says will you wait here, sir, until they send for you.'

'O.K. How long have they been at it?'

'About twenty minutes so far.'

For a further fifteen minutes Manton and the inspector conducted a desultory conversation which held little interest for either of them.

Then, suddenly a door marked 'Private' opened and Andrews came out. He appeared surprised to see Manton, frowned slightly and passed outside to join the growing throng of spectators. A minute later the same door opened again and a small man who had the appearance of a city bank manager beckoned to Manton.

Feeling not unlike Alice in pursuit of the White Rabbit, Manton found himself following him down a long passage which ran beside the court-room. By the time he reached the end, the man had vanished, but a second later Manton spotted him holding open a door. He waited for Manton to enter, then closed it and with remarkable deftness of movement skipped round to his seat at the far end of a large green baize table. To Manton's right and with their backs to the window sat the four magistrates. He felt their combined stare on him as though he might be an emissary from outer space. The man who had fetched Manton turned out to be Mr. Ellis himself, and he now addressed Manton in a dry, matter-of-fact voice.

'As I believe you are aware, Superintendent, the magistrates have under consideration an application by Mr. George Andrews for a warrant against one Bernard Kingston on a charge of murdering Susan Andrews.' He paused to fix his gaze on Manton, who had been left standing at the corner of the table nearest the door and farthest from the other occupants of the room. Apparently satisfied that he had so far made himself clear he picked up a slender bundle of papers. 'In support of his application, Mr. Andrews has submitted statements by persons whom he is ready to call before the magistrates if required, and on whose evidence, he suggests, his application should be granted. Amongst the statements, I note there is what might perhaps be called an abstract of your evidence.'

'My evidence?' Manton exclaimed.

Mr. Ellis nodded. 'I somehow thought you might not be aware of it, but, as I say, it doesn't purport to be a signed statement, just a summary of what Mr. Andrews thinks you could testify to, if necessary.'

'I see,' Manton said without enthusiasm.

'Now then,' the clerk went on. 'There are one or two points on which the magistrates would like to have your assistance in reaching their decision on this application.'

Manton switched his gaze to the four magistrates who had been impassively watching him since he came into the room. They might, from their expressions, have been directors at a rather tense board meeting. For the most part, heads were supported by hands and bottoms were given over to frequent squirming. Lady Neale alone sat quite still, exhibiting a bird-like alertness beneath a toque of green and mauve petals which looked as though it might at any moment slip right down over her face. Manton brought his attention back to the clerk, who, after studying a small sheet of paper in his hand, began to speak again.

'In the first place, the magistrates would like to know whether your inquiries are still proceeding.'

'Most certainly they are.'

Mr. Ellis pencilled a tick on the sheet of paper.

'With a definite suspect in mind?'

'Ye-es, I think I can say that.'

'Remembering that we are sitting in private and that there's no question of the Press knowing what passes in this room, perhaps you'd even like to say whether your suspect is the same person against whom Mr. Andrews is seeking a warrant?'

'It is the same person.'

Mr. Ellis made a further tick.

And I know what you're going to ask next, Manton felt like saying when the clerk looked up again.

'Can you give the magistrates any estimate of your hopes regarding an arrest?'

'I certainly hope to make one.'

Mr. Ellis smiled thinly. 'I dare say, but how well grounded are your hopes? What we want to know is whether you expect to make an arrest in the reasonably near future?'

Manton became aware that all squirming had

abruptly ceased and that he was the subject of an intense scrutiny by five pairs of eyes. He realised that on his answer might well depend the outcome of Andrews's application, for he had been made to realise for some time past that there was quite a body of opinion in favour of Kingston's immediate arrest. For aught he knew, the four magistrates might share that view.

'I can only say, sir, that I hope it won't be long before an arrest is made.'

'You're referring to Kingston?' Mr. Ellis asked, with lawyer's caution.

Manton nodded and with a small sigh the clerk laid down his sheet of paper and looked down the line of magistrates.

'Are there any questions you'd like to put to the officer?' he asked, glancing from face to face.

It was Lady Neale who immediately spoke. 'I'd like to know whether this man Kingston is your *only* suspect, Superintendent,' she said in a forbidding voice.

There was a tense silence while Manton chewed his lower lip and transferred his hat from one hand to the other. Without looking in her direction, he replied, 'He is the chief suspect, madam.'

'May we be informed of the names of any other suspects?'

The atmosphere became more electric, for

Manton could tell from the expressions on the faces of the other magistrates and their clerk that they were well aware of the import of Lady Neale's questions, and were probably wondering anxiously whether they might not find themselves suddenly caught up in a highly explosive situation.

Addressing himself exclusively to Mr. Ellis, Manton said, 'I don't think, sir, that I ought to be asked to divulge the names of possible other suspects.'

To his relief he saw the chairman nod vigorously and heard him whisper fiercely at his fellow magistrates, 'Won't help us. He's told us Kingston is the main suspect and that his inquiries are still continuing. I don't see we need keep him any longer.'

The corners of Lady Neale's mouth turned down in angry disapproval but she remained silent.

Ten minutes later the magistrates made their entry into what was by then an overflowing court, with people squeezed into every available space. In the general confusion a number of reporters had even taken possession of the dock from which they had resolutely declined to be dislodged.

'Mr. Andrews?' the clerk called out when relative quiet had been imposed. George Andrews stepped forward and stood in front of Mr. Ellis. The chairman put on his spectacles with a good deal of nervous fumbling and picked up a large sheet of stiff paper from which he proceeded to read.

'The magistrates have given the most careful consideration to the application for a warrant for murder which has just been made to them by Mr. Andrews. The magistrates feel that it would be unwise, if not improper, for them to say more at this stage than that they reject the application.'

There was a moment of frozen silence, and then Andrews made a small, formal bow before turning and making his way out of court followed in an eager scramble by the Press. Two of the reporters who had secured themselves in the dock actually vaulted over the side in their determination not to be left behind, this gymnastic act being made necessary by the retaliatory action of the court inspector who, failing to evict them in time, had locked them in.

Manton cast a quick look round the emptying court to see if there was any sign of Kingston himself. There was not, though this scarcely surprised him since he had thought it unlikely that he would appear in the circumstances. It would have been rather like the fox mingling with the hounds and huntsmen at the start of a meet. He glanced at his watch and saw that it was shortly after half-past eleven. He decided to pick up Avis and drive over to Woodford to visit Mrs. Kingston. Her husband would most likely be out, and though Detective-Sergeant Hay had taken a short statement from her two days previously, he had always had it in mind to see her himself. Even though she could never be called as a witness for the prosecution against her husband, it was often useful to tie down the husbands or wives of suspects to one story so that they couldn't readily say something entirely different at a later stage.

It was only as they drove into Woodford that it occurred to Manton that their arrival might coincide with the girls being home from school for lunch. He mentioned the possibility to Avis, who merely shrugged and said in that event they'd just have to drive around until they'd left again.

Luck, however, was with them, for not only were the girls not at home, but Peggy Kingston was. Moreover, she was alone. She showed them into the same room in which her husband had received them in the middle of the night, but whereas on that occasion Manton had scarcely noticed anything about the room beyond an enormous television set squatting incongruously in one corner, this time he looked about him with unhurried interest. The television set, clearly one of Yander's latest models, still filled the same corner of the room, and against the wall next to it was an equally resplendent combined radio and record-player.

These two items succeeded in drawing attention to the no less modern though rather less fancy nature of the remaining furniture, which comprised a coffee table with a couple of women's magazines on it and a matching settee and two chairs upholstered in dung-coloured whipcord. At Peggy Kingston's invitation, Manton and Avis took the two chairs while she perched herself nervously on the edge of the settee.

'May I assume, Mrs. Kingston, that you know the general purpose of my visit?'

'About my husband and that girl's death, is it?'

Manton nodded, surprised by the directness of her reply. 'You know that he is under suspicion?'

She looked down at her hands which were clasped in her lap. 'Yes,' she said in a whisper.

'Anything you can do to help clear him must be to his advantage. It will also assist the police. That's why I'm here.'

'Or is it because you hope I'll incriminate him?' she asked, her mouth trembling.

Ignoring the reproach, Manton went on, 'I wonder if you could be more exact about the time he arrived home on Friday evening, or rather on Saturday morning? You told Sergeant Hay when he visited you a few days ago that it was some time after midnight, but that you couldn't be more specific. Do you think it might have been around one o'clock or two o'clock or perhaps even later?' As he spoke, Manton wondered whether he had indicated a shade too much eagerness about the answer he hoped for.

'I'm sure it was nearer midnight than one o'clock,' she replied.

Manton felt crestfallen. If Susan had been murdered some time between midnight and half-past, it would have taken Kingston at least an hour to drive from Offing to Woodford, which would have meant, if he were the murderer, that he could not have reached home before half-past one at the earliest.

'Why are you now sure of that?' he asked. 'Previously you told Sergeant Hay that you couldn't fix the hour at all.'

'I've thought about it more since then.' As she spoke her eyes challenged Manton's.

'What time had you gone to bed on Friday evening?' he asked, in a tone which was still quiet and friendly.

'I don't remember exactly, but around eleven I believe.'

'And had you fallen asleep before your husband returned?'

'Yes.'

'What was the first you knew of his return?'

'When he walked into the bedroom.'

'Did you get out of bed?'

'No.'

'Was the light on?'

'Yes.'

'Who switched it on?'

'My husband did when he saw I'd woken up.'

Manton observed that she was taking pains to avoid looking at him. It was apparent that whatever domestic recriminations had taken place, there had been agreement to present a united front to the police.

'Did you notice he had a scratch on his face?'

'I believe he mentioned it.'

'Did he tell you how he'd got it?'

'No.'

'But you doubtless asked him?'

She shook her head. 'No! It didn't seem very important at that hour of the night. I just assumed he had caught the side of his face against something sharp.'

Manton leaned forward and said keenly, 'But surely, if he mentioned it, Mrs. Kingston, he must have explained how he came by it?'

'He may have done, but I don't remember. Anyway, I was half asleep.'

'And was it because you had been half asleep that you told Sergeant Hay you had no idea what time your husband came in?'

There was a tense pause while Peggy Kingston apparently contemplated the chasm into which Manton's next question seemed likely to topple her.

'I'm still sure it was only just after midnight

when he came in,' she said desperately.

'That wasn't what I asked you,' he said quietly. 'But, anyway, why are you now so sure?'

'I remember noticing the time by the clock on my bedside table.'

'Why didn't you tell Sergeant Hay that? Why did you tell him you didn't know the time your husband came in except that it was some time after midnight?'

Slowly she licked each corner of her mouth where the lipstick was in need of repair, and then looking him full in the face she said, 'I'm quite prepared to go into the witness-box and swear that my husband was home very shortly after midnight.'

CHAPTER TWENTY-TWO

When Bernard Kingston returned home around seven o'clock that evening, his wife was still sitting on the edge of the sofa, where Manton and Avis had left her several hours before. She had not, in truth, remained there the whole time. Indeed, she had only just gone back into the room, leaving her daughters frowning over their homework in the kitchen, when she heard the front-door open.

'Where's Mummy?' she heard him ask in the

kitchen a minute later. His tone was suspicious, for normally she would have been there preparing supper in between bouts of exhorting Sylvia and Deirdre to get on with their homework.

'She went out just now,' Deirdre answered in a preoccupied voice.

'Out of the house, do you mean?'

There was no audible reply, and a second later she heard him out in the hall.

'Where are you, Peggy?'

'In here.'

He came to the door and looked in.

'Having a rest?' he asked in a hearty tone. 'What sort of a day have you had?'

'The police were here this afternoon, Bernard,' she said slowly.

'That Superintendent fellow from the Yard?' His tone was anxious.

'Yes.'

'What did you tell him?'

'Why do you ask what I told him in that voice, instead of what he asked me?'

'I can guess what he asked you,' he replied grimly. 'About what time I arrived home last Friday and how I appeared and all that; am I right?'

'Yes.'

'So what did you tell him?' When she didn't reply immediately: 'Peggy, what did you tell him?'

She looked abruptly away from him before replying in a bitter tone, 'It's all right, you needn't worry. I told him you came in soon after midnight. That was what you wanted me to say, wasn't it!'

He expelled his breath in a long sigh while he continued to watch his wife with a puzzled expression. 'What's wrong with you, Peggy? Did he cut up nasty and upset you? If so, I'll—'

'I lie to the police to save your skin,' she broke in, 'and you ask what's wrong with me!'

'Oh, come, Peggy, it wasn't exactly lying,' he said in a coaxing voice, at the same time softly closing the door. 'It might have been lying if I had murdered the girl. As it is, it's no more than . . . than, well, trying to save everyone a bit of embarrassment, including the police. After all, since I'm not their man, the sooner I'm cleared, the better.' His voice assumed an aggrieved note. 'It's damnable that I should have fallen under suspicion in this way.'

While he had been speaking, his wife had been looking at him in growing disbelief. 'You really are quite remarkable, aren't you?'

'I don't know what you mean.'

'The way you apparently expect everyone to be as convinced of your innocence as you pretend to be yourself.'

'But, Peggy, I am innocent. I didn't murder Susan. You know that.'

'I don't know what to believe.'

'You can't doubt your own husband,' he exclaimed, this time with a note of indignation creeping into his tone.

'There you go again! Why can't I doubt you? Is your record as a husband such that you consider I have no cause for doubt?'

'You're upset, Peggy. Why don't you go and lie down?'

She appeared not to hear him as she went on, 'God knows I wish I didn't have cause for doubt, but the brutal truth is, Bernard, that I don't trust you any more. You've lied too often about all your sordid little affairs. In the end, you scarcely even bothered to make your lies convincing ones; I suppose you thought I wasn't worth the trouble.'

Kingston gazed at his wife with an expression of stupefied amazement which slowly gave way to one of affronted dignity.

'If that's the way you feel,' he said stiffly, 'I don't know why you bothered to lie, as you put it, to the police. If I matter so little to you, why didn't you tell them I didn't come home that night until after two o'clock? And for good measure you could have added that you personally believed I was a murderer.'

'I'll tell you why,' she replied through tight lips. 'Most husbands would know without asking, but not you. I lied for the sake of the girls, for the sake of our families, even for the sake of the neighbours. I never knew Susan

Andrews and nothing I can now say or do will bring her back to life. All I can try to do is keep our home together, at least for a few more years until the children have grown up. That's why I lied to the police: it wasn't because I believed you were innocent. I don't know whether you are or not. You took the girl out and you doubtless made one of your famous passes at her, but whether or not you killed her is for me in one sense unimportant.' She brushed aside his protest. 'I'm prepared to fight in order to protect our children and our families from the shame and degradation and utter destruction of all our lives which would inevitably follow your arrest. That's why I lied; that's why I'd lie again, not with any pleasure, but as the lesser of two evils which threaten to engulf us.' She cast him a look of contempt. 'So you can breathe again, Bernard, I won't let you down. I'll even lie for you, though not perhaps out of the most flattering motives.'

'My God, how you must hate me!' he said in a stunned voice.

'No, I don't. You've long since killed any love I ever felt for you, but I don't hate you.'

'But I need you, Peggy, now more than ever. I need your trust.' He went on vehemently, 'Do you realise what's been happening this very day? The dead girl's father has been trying to obtain a warrant for my arrest over the heads of the police. I'm being persecuted, Peggy. You must give me your trust and believe in me. Please, darling.'

She shook her head very slowly. 'Don't fool yourself; this isn't the return of the prodigal, just a glib piece of death-bed repentance. I've told you I'll stick by you. Be satisfied with that, but don't expect me to open my arms to you.' She rose to her feet and gave a little shiver as though she were suddenly cold. 'I must go and prepare supper, also see how the girls are getting on with their homework. Incidentally, strange though it may seem, they have no idea as yet that their father is a suspected murderer. I pray only that they'll remain in ignorance.'

As she moved to leave the room, he put out an appealing hand, but she brushed past him as though he was no longer there.

*   *   *

Michael Neale had just finished dinner in hall and was contemplating how to pass the evening when a message reached him that he was wanted on the telephone. He walked briskly across the main court to the porter's lodge, which was the only place in college where undergraduates could make and receive calls, and shut himself into the glass-panelled booth which smelt permanently of stale night-club and railway station urinal.

'Michael Neale here,' he said with the slight

wariness engendered by an unexpected telephone call. Any hopes he might have entertained were, however, dashed when he heard his mother's voice on the line.

'Hello, darling, how are you?'

'I'm all right, and you?'

'Splendid.'

'And Father?'

'Yes, he's fine too.' The civilities out of the way, she went on in a rush, 'Will you be coming over on Saturday or Sunday?'

'I hadn't intended to. Anyway, I'm behind with my work and I ought to try to catch up a bit.'

'I hope you're not working too hard, darling, you'll only make yourself ill.'

'I've a long way to go before there's any danger of that,' he remarked with a hollow laugh.

'Why don't you drive over for lunch on Sunday?'

'Any special reason?'

'Darling, don't sound so suspicious. We just want to see you.'

'Well, I don't think I'll be able to. As I say, I shall probably have to work most of Sunday. One gets sent down for not working these days. It's not like when Father was up.' He realised that his mother was trying to manoeuvre an opening in order to reveal the real purpose of her call, but he became suddenly revolted by the atmosphere in the call-box and determined to cut short their conversation. 'Was there anything else, Mother? Otherwise I must go.'

'Tell me, darling, have the police been to see you again? About that friend of yours whose death they were investigating. You never mentioned it again.'

'I haven't heard anything more,' he replied flatly.

There was a small, exasperated sigh at the other end of the line. 'I'm afraid I must ask you to be frank with me, Michael; you see, I happen to know that those two officers who came to the house on Saturday evening are the ones who are investigating Susan Andrew's death. Was it because they'd been told you used to know her that they came?'

'Since you seem to know anyway, why do you ask?'

'Look, Michael,' she said in a tone of asperity, 'I must insist that you're frank with me over this. You haven't been so far and it's—well, it's rather hurtful, but you must tell me exactly what the police wanted to know.'

'They wished me to tell them when I'd last seen Susan,' he said in a defiant voice.

'And of course you told them you'd had nothing to do with her since last summer?'

'Of course.'

To his own ears, his tone sounded childishly ironical, but Lady Neale, from her next

202

remark, seemed to have accepted the reassurance at face value.

'Darling, you could have saved me so much worry if you'd told me all this at the outset instead of behaving like a small martyred schoolboy.' She paused. 'I expect you've seen an evening paper?'

'No, I haven't.'

'Then you won't have read how Mr. Andrews applied to the court this morning for a warrant for the arrest of someone in connection with his daughter's death.'

'What happened?' Neale asked, with quickening interest.

'I'm afraid he went away disappointed, though there's absolutely no doubt that both he and the police are after the right man. But I mustn't keep you. Do try to come for lunch on Sunday, darling, and I'll tell you all I've heard about the case. The village is full of rumours; it seems she wasn't a very moral sort of girl.'

It was perhaps fortunate that Lady Neale was unable to see such colour as he ever had drain from her son's face at this last remark. A second later she had rung off, leaving him leaning against the wall of the call-box and taking a series of deep breaths in an endeavour to regain his composure. It was at least two minutes before he felt able to leave his sanctuary and walk across the court to his room, where he locked the door and flung himself down on his bed. How dared his own mother of all people quote a piece of filthy village gossip! How dared she or anyone else try and besmirch his memory of Susan!

Slowly his breathing became normal again, his mind cleared and he began to give some practical thought to his position. He realised that Manton still regarded him with suspicion, but he supposed this was inevitable in the light of police knowledge of the clandestine affair which he and Susan had carried on. He had done his best to persuade Manton of his innocence, and happily his own conscience was clear, so all he could do was sit back and await the passing of the shadow.

Nevertheless, he hoped that it wouldn't be too long before they dug up enough evidence to arrest Kingston—he had only recently learnt the man's name—for one could never be certain that some wily newspaper mightn't decide to inject fresh interest into the case by artfully introducing his, Neale's, name in association with the dead girl's. Anything of that nature and life would become a nightmare—an insupportable nightmare so far as continued existence at Cambridge was concerned.

No, the sooner Kingston was arrested the better. A pity his mother and her fellow magistrates hadn't seen fit to authorise that when Mr. Andrews had made his application. It had all sounded cock-eyed, but if any private citizen could apply, as his mother had explained, to have another arrested, why shouldn't he have had a stab at getting Kingston behind bars. He must find out more about it. Perhaps he would drive home for lunch on Sunday, after all. But there suddenly arose before his eyes a clear picture of the occasion. There would be a completely general conversation over the meal, but as soon as his father had retired to his study for a siesta, his mother would begin one of her pitiless, probing cross-examinations.

On further thought, it was better to leave others to arrange for Kingston's arrest and to keep out of his mother's way for the time being. So thinking, he rolled off the bed and moodily started to undress.

★   ★   ★

'Ready?' George Andrews stood with one hand on the light switch while he watched his wife, who was sitting bolt upright in bed, gently close her Bible and lay it carefully on the bedside table. Since Susan's funeral, she had taken to reading it assiduously each night. She had begun to do so without comment and he, in turn, had not remarked on the habit. He was glad enough that she managed to derive solace from her reading. Anything to help her through the trance-like state she had been in since

Susan's death.

In answer to his question, she slithered down between the bedclothes until only her head was showing. Andrews turned off the light then moved across to open the window before taking off his dressing-gown and getting into bed. For a few seconds there was complete stillness in the room, then Winnie Andrews spoke.

'What's going to happen now, George?'

'About the case, do you mean?'

'Yes, now that the court has refused to give you your warrant.'

'All I can do is wait a short time to see what Manton does. If he doesn't make an arrest within the next week, I'll start agitating again. I can either stir up the Press or write to our M.P., saying I'm dissatisfied with the manner in which the whole investigation has been conducted, or I can press for the coroner to resume his inquest. I might even do all three.'

'But if the police don't arrest anyone, what can the coroner do?' she asked in a feebly bewildered tone.

'If he does his job properly, he'll see that the jury returns a verdict of murder against Kingston. And if that happens, Kingston is automatically committed for trial at the Assizes, without there having to be the usual hearing before the magistrates.'

'I see, but supposing it doesn't work out the way you want, what are you going to do then?'

'Time enough to decide that later.' A short silence followed before he said dreamily, 'If only I could discover just one damning piece of evidence against Kingston which I could put to him at the inquest, something which the police and everyone has overlooked, my God I'd make them all look fools.' He paused. 'I've got to find something.'

'You'd better go to sleep now, George, or you won't feel ready for work in the morning.'

'I'm not going to work in the morning, I've arranged to take a week's leave. If the police won't do their job properly, I'm going to have to become a detective again to solve my own daughter's death.'

CHAPTER TWENTY-THREE

Manton had just arrived at Offing Police Station the next morning when a telephone call came through from the Chief Constable. He sounded agitated and lost no time in coming to the point.

'I've been informed that Andrews is about to go off and do some detective work on his own.'

'I hadn't heard that, sir, though it doesn't surprise me.'

'Well, it does embarrass me, one of my ex-detective-inspectors trying to show us up. And don't underestimate him either, he's a

207

tenacious fellow.'

'I already know that, sir,' Manton remarked sardonically. 'But there's nothing I can do to prevent him.'

'You must try to get ahead of him, anticipate what he's up to and do it first.'

Manton raised his eyes to the ceiling in silent despair. In a grating tone, he said, 'I'm not proposing, sir, to follow him around like a bloodhound. If he does uncover any fresh evidence, it's his duty to let me know. I'll tell him that, but I don't see what else I can do.'

'Well, do what you like, but don't say I haven't warned you. I'm not at all happy, Manton, not at all happy. Any moment we're likely to be made utter fools. It's too late now, but we ought to have arrested and charged Kingston before Andrews ever stepped into the picture. Nobody could have said we didn't have quite a bit of evidence against him and my own personal opinion is that we should have got a committal for trial.'

'Only to see him walk out a free man at the Assizes, sir,' Manton said firmly.

'Better that than never have him there at all.'

It seemed to Manton that their conversation might continue in sterile circles till one of them gave up.

'Well, sir, I'll see Andrews this morning and meanwhile keep you informed of developments.'

'Let's just hope there are some.'

When Avis looked in a few minutes later, Manton said, 'The Chief's got the wind up, Dick. Any moment he's going to pass a great big public vote of no confidence in my conduct of the inquiry. It'll all be prettily wrapped up, of course, but the meaning will be there all right.'

He gave Avis a report on his recent telephone conversation and then said, 'I suppose I'd better phone Andrews at once, before he puts on his deer-stalker and goes out.'

Though his tone was flippant, he felt less than cheerful. He was still further from that state after he had made the call, for Andrews flatly declined to give any indication or undertaking as to what he would do if he uncovered fresh evidence. It was with a sense of mounting frustration that Manton rang off and stared out of the window of Newbold's tiny office. He felt like an animal in a zoo which has never known any wider horizon.

At this moment he was ready to throw in his hand and take a boat up the Amazon, from where better men than he had not returned.

★   ★   ★

In the two weeks which followed, there remained one small crystal of solace in an otherwise debilitating situation. It was that

George Andrews appeared to be having no greater success with his inquiries than Manton himself. Despite his having told the Chief Constable that he didn't intend to follow Andrews about like a bloodhound, Manton had nevertheless made it his business to keep an eye on him and have at least a general notion what he was up to. So far all he had done was to interview all the lay witnesses whom Manton or one of his team had already seen.

All, that is, save for Kingston, though this had not been for want of effort. He had, so Manton was soon informed, tried on two occasions to gain admittance to the Kingston home but each time had had the door peremptorily shut in his face. On a further occasion he had endeavoured to waylay Mrs. Kingston in the street, but she had refused to speak to him and had threatened to summon a policeman if he didn't remove himself from her path.

But while this had all been going on, Manton himself had failed to make a single further inch of progress in the inquiry. He felt like someone standing in a wide open space from which every line of egress has proved to be a cul-de-sac. The momentum of the inquiry was dissipated, frustration and disillusionment had set in like some fearful atrophy. Manton was now amongst those whose opinion was that Kingston should have been arrested at once. Anything would

have been better than the existing stalemate.
Moreover, in a murder investigation it behoves
the police never to close their books, if not until
the case has been solved, at least before the
public is ready to accept failure. This can mean
that desultory inquiries must continue and that
the officer in charge must spend an increasing
amount of time in re-reading all the statements
which have been taken and in attending
smoke-laden conferences which finish as they
begin with weary hopelessness.

And yet Manton knew as well as any other
senior detective that the slog had to continue.
That the statements must be read a fifth and a
sixth . . . and a hundredth time. That the key
witnesses must be further interviewed and then
once more again, for only this way lay any hope
at all. In his heart of hearts he realised that, like
the first snowdrop, something might suddenly
appear in the barren landscape which would set
him off along the home-run.

The frustration of the last two weeks had
been enhanced by the beauty of the weather.
One glorious spring day had succeeded another,
and such showers as there had been had
dutifully come at night. Indeed, to look out of
the window or to stroll down Offing's main
street had made him more sharply aware of his
own unco-operative presence in the midst of
nature's triumph. He had always felt that
weather should match his mood, in the same

way that background music reflects that of a film. At the moment, however, it was like the blending of a Mozart melody with a Tennessee Williams plot of unleashed realism.

It was early one morning soon after he had reached the station that a call came through from the Yard and a voice said: 'The A.C.C. would like to see you as soon as you can make it, Mr. Manton.'

CHAPTER TWENTY-FOUR

During the ten minutes that he sat waiting in the A.C.C.'s outer office, Manton had time to brace himself for the interview ahead. Of all the possibilities, it seemed to him most likely that he was going to be taken off the inquiry in deference to the Chief Constable, who, he surmised, had finally asked for his recall. If this was so, it would not only be a blow to his self-esteem but a black mark on his service record. The chance of further promotion to Chief Superintendent and even to Commander would be diminished, and he would have to keep his eye open for a job outside. They were certainly to be had, and good ones too; moreover, there was small doubt that Marjorie, his wife, would be delighted at the prospect of having a husband with regular hours and free week-ends.

The A.C.C.'s secretary broke in on his thoughts: 'He's free now.'

Manton got up, automatically straightened his tie and knocked on the inner door.

'Sorry to have kept you waiting, Simon. Just had the Home Office on the phone about this case of yours.' Manton assumed an expression of polite interest. 'Andrews has been agitating again. He's lit a fire under his M.P., who in turn has submitted a pile of documents to the Home Secretary, who wants to know what we're going to do. I told him I'd let him know after I'd had a word with you.' He ran his tongue round his mouth as though in search of some missing crumbs of breakfast. 'I take it you've no fresh evidence?'

'I'm afraid not, sir.'

'I'm almost beginning to think it's a pity we didn't arrest Kingston straight away, but it's too late now unless we dig up something new against him.'

'I feel the same way myself, sir.'

'I've tried to protect you from the fringe distractions. If I hadn't, you'd have spent the whole of every day writing reports and answering a lot of damned silly questions by people who are not especially interested in the answers. They just like asking the questions.'

'I'm afraid the Chief Constable isn't satisfied with the way things have gone.'

'Don't know what he has to grumble about! It's we who carry the can for any failure, not he. However, the position is this, I saw the Director last night and after a lengthy discussion of the various courses open to us, we decided in the light of continuing pressure from Andrews—and of course he now has the whole national Press backing him up, the undaunted father fighting single-handed for justice and all that tripe—that the coroner should be asked to resume his inquest and carry it through to completion. His jury are bound to bring in a verdict of murder either against some person unknown or against Kingston, depending on how they feel about the evidence, or more probably on how much rope the coroner gives them.'

'And what part do the police play in this, sir?'

'You hand the coroner a copy of your complete file and leave him to call all the evidence he wishes. Unofficially, you can suggest he calls the lot; that is, everyone who can say anything remotely material to the case.'

'He'll be bound to call Kingston, sir.'

'Of course he will, but I imagine Kingston will have a solicitor there, and how far his evidence will get before the inevitable warning about not being obliged to answer any question which may incriminate him remains to be seen. His solicitor will probably be quick to nudge the coroner when it reaches the point.' He looked at Manton over the top of his spectacles. 'Well, what do you think about it?'

'At least it means doing something, sir, instead of trying to fight our way out of a barrel of treacle. Who knows, something fresh may come to light. On the other hand it's a pretty good admission that I've fallen down on the job. The inquest is normally resumed only when the police have had considerably longer than I've had and still not made an arrest.'

'Yes, but I've explained the reason for the present action is outside pressure. And this'll be good for the public.'

These last words continued to ring in Manton's ears as he drove back to Offing later the same morning. Good for the public maybe, but certainly not good for Detective-Superintendent Manton who felt he was being deftly prepared for the sacrificial altar.

CHAPTER TWENTY-FIVE

It was a further five days before Mr. Kerslake, the coroner, resumed the inquest. News of the impending event had the effect of resuscitating newspaper interest in the case, and those who actually received notices to attend as witnesses experienced the glowing excitement of guests invited to a royal wedding. All save one that is, since Kingston's reaction had been one of blustering resentment.

Manton had expected Mr. Kerslake to summon him for a conference after he had read and digested the police file. He was indeed sent for by the coroner, but only to be handed a list of witnesses with the request that they should be warned to present themselves punctually at half-past ten on the appointed day.

With the actual day there also arrived two television cameras and a reinforced guard of newspaper reporters. As Manton stepped out of his car, Sankey of the *Morning Herald* materialised at his side and said with one of his faintly mocking smiles, 'Well, Superintendent, are we in for some surprises?'

'I'm not the person to ask, why not try your friend Andrews?'

Sankey shook his head sadly.

'You might have solved this case weeks ago if you'd been a little more co-operative with the Press. I'm not saying you would have, but you might have.'

This brief conversation served to increase the edginess which Manton was already feeling and which was not further helped by the Roman Circus atmosphere he found inside Mr. Kerslake's court. He thrust his way through to the front.

'For heaven's sake let's have some windows open,' he called across to the coroner's officer who was blowing the dust off the testament to be used by the witnesses.

'Every one that'll open is open,' the officer replied laconically.

Manton made a despairing face and laid his file on the lawyer's table next to Mr. Thirkell's briefcase. So the Neales were being represented again!

A short, grey-haired man with a fiercely aggressive expression came up to him. 'Are you Superintendent Manton by any chance?'

'I am.'

'My name's Denny. I'm a solicitor, representing Mr. Kingston.'

'I assumed he'd have someone here on his behalf,' Manton remarked.

Mr. Denny grunted. 'I don't mind telling you that I shan't be pulling my punches either. I don't care that'—he snapped his fingers with the noise of a rifle being discharged—'for coroners. Most of them are vain or incompetent.'

'I don't think you'll find Mr. Kerslake in either category.'

'We'll see.' His gaze went up and down Manton. 'I'm not afraid of attacking the police either when occasion demands.'

Their conversation was interrupted by the appearance of Mr. Thirkell. Mr. Denny gave him a sharp, appraising look and moved away to the far end of the table.

Mr. Thirkell grinned amiably. 'Who was that little terrier?' Manton told him. 'Ho-ho! So we're going to have some fun, are we? I can just see him behaving like a Chinese cracker.'

'All the witnesses are now here, sir,' Avis announced, coming up on Manton's other side.

'Thanks, Dick. Keep 'em quiet and see they don't start granting television interviews or there'll be hell to pay.'

When Mr. Kerslake entered and took his seat in the small court-room, which on a sunny day still managed to look depressingly drab in its various shades of sweating brown, the atmosphere resembled that of a survival shelter whose air conditioning has failed. He gazed about him with an expression of distaste, though whether this was occasioned more by the foetid air than by the rows of expectant faces remained unresolved since he vouchsafed no oral comment. He opened a fat notebook, carefully smoothed the page, and then resting his folded hands on it addressed himself to the twelve anxious faces on his right.

'Members of the jury, we are here to resume the inquest into the death of Susan Andrews. When you have heard all the evidence, together with my summing-up, it will be your duty to return a verdict on how this girl came to meet her death. Let me emphasise that your duty is to decide just that: namely, how did she die? Was it as a result of murder, of manslaughter, or was it a case of death by misadventure? If you decide that it was murder, your verdict should additionally record whether it was by some person unknown, which would mean that there was not sufficient evidence to satisfy you who killed her, or whether it was murder by a person whom you name in your verdict.' His glance roamed the court as though to indicate that no one should count himself safe from the accusing finger. It came to rest on Mr. Denny, who glared back at him. 'In order to return the latter verdict, you would have to be satisfied by the evidence that such a person had committed the crime. But let me remind you again that your prime function is to decide how Susan Andrews met her death. No one stands before you charged with any offence in connection with it. In this court'—he made a sweeping gesture with his hand—'there is no accused sitting in the dock. There isn't even a dock.' He turned to study his notebook. 'And now we will have the first witness. Call Dr. Ryman.'

Before the pathologist could reach the witness-box, however, Mr. Denny had sprung to his feet.

'I should be glad to know, sir, when you propose calling my client, Mr. Kingston?'

'Later,' Mr. Kerslake replied coldly. 'I can't tell you when.'

'It would be a matter of great convenience if you could indicate his place in the list.'

219

'Why do you wish to know? If you're watching these proceedings on his behalf, you'll presumably be here all the time, so what difference does it make to you when he's called?'

'As a matter of courtesy, I should like to know,' Mr. Denny retorted haughtily.

Mr. Kerslake gave a sudden sigh. 'Do you think I might be allowed to proceed now?' he asked in a sweetly reasonable tone which was designed to isolate Mr. Denny and show him up for the squalid nuisance Mr. Kerslake saw him to be. Mr. Denny sat down and wrote in his notebook in letters which could almost be read from the far side of the court, the words, 'This coroner is both offensive and incompetent.'

Meanwhile, Dr. Ryman had reached the witness-box and taken the oath. For a second or two he and Mr. Kerslake regarded each other like a couple of boxers waiting for the first round.

'Do you hand in a copy of your report?' Mr. Kerslake asked with prim formality.

'Yes, here you are,' the pathologist replied breezily, 'with some spares as well.' He glanced round the court with the keen air of a newsvendor.

The next few minutes were spent in the report being read aloud, after which Mr. Kerslake looked toward the two solicitors. 'Any questions to ask this witness?'

Mr. Thirkell shook his head but Mr. Denny was immediately on his feet.

'Did your examination of this girl's body and clothing, Doctor, provide any indication as to *who* had murdered her, assuming that she *was* murdered?'

Dr. Ryman puffed out his cheeks and shook his shaggy head in a gesture of mild exasperation.

'If you mean by that, was it someone called Smith or Jones, the answer is that there wasn't any indication as to the person's identity. On the other hand, from the composite picture I formed, I would say that it was certainly a male and that he was in possession of a towel. For some reason at which one can only guess, he placed the towel over her head while he was strangling her. That would account for the piece of cotton I found caught between her two front teeth. You'll be hearing from the laboratory witness that the fragment of cotton almost certainly did come from a towel.' He smiled benignly at Mr. Denny. 'So you see, I would say there was indication to that extent.'

Mr. Denny, whose impatience with the reply had been visibly growing, now said in a withering tone, 'So what it amounts to is this, that the murder could have been committed by any one of the thirty million males in this country—apart from the few who may not own towels?' He sat down under Dr. Ryman's reproachful gaze.

The coroner was about to dismiss the witness when George Andrews stepped forward. 'I should like to ask Dr. Ryman a question, sir.'

'As father of the dead girl?' Mr. Kerslake asked punctiliously.

'Yes.'

'Very well.'

'Is it a fact that my daughter was a virgin at the time of her death?'

'You asked that last time,' Mr. Kerslake broke in. 'We already have his answer.'

'I'd like to hear it again, sir,' Andrews said firmly. He had had his hair close-cropped, and this added to the general severity of his appearance as he confronted coroner and witness.

Dr. Ryman looked at him with an almost paternal expression. 'As I've said in my report, there was no evidence that your lass had ever indulged in full sexual intercourse.'

Andrews bit his lip and appeared to be about to ask a further question. Then he muttered, 'That's all, thank you,' and stepped back into his seat.

'Are you satisfied now?' Mr. Kerslake asked.

Andrews straightened on the verge of sitting down. 'I am, sir.' He looked challengingly round the court. 'And I hope the whole of Offing is as well.'

Deciding apparently that this was an

indiscretion which was better ignored, Mr. Kerslake said, 'Now call Edward Kitchener Champigny.'

A rather faded, weary-looking man with a pink folder under his arm made his tortuous way to the witness-box, took the oath and admitted to Mr. Kerslake that he was a scientific officer at the Metropolitan Police Laboratory at Scotland Yard. He then proceeded to give his evidence which amounted to little more than a succession of negatives in respect of the various garments and specimens he had examined. In regard to the thread found between Susan's teeth, he testified that it was in every way similar to the threads found in white towelling. Further than that, he said with a sad flickering smile, he couldn't go. When it came to questions, Mr. Denny was as usual first on his feet.

'Did you find anything at all connecting Mr. Kingston with the crime?' he barked.

'No.'

'Amongst other things, did you examine sweepings which purported to have come from Mr. Kingston's car?'

'I did.'

'Did you find a single speck of anything suggesting that the girl had met her death in that car?'

'I did not.'

With a brisk, satisfied nod, Mr. Denny sat

down, and Mr. Thirkell having shaken his head, Andrews rose.

'Did it appear from my daughter's blouse that she had been involved in a struggle?'

Mr. Champigny smiled wanly. 'All I can say is that a button was missing from her blouse and that it appeared to have been torn off. I don't think it's for me to draw the inference that it came off in a struggle.'

'But do you agree that is the way most buttons come off?'

The witness raised his eyebrows in mild surprise. 'I can't really say I do.'

'What are you trying to show by your questions?' Mr. Kerslake asked in a voice of judicial detachment.

'That my daughter put up a fight for her honour.'

'Well, now that the jury have heard that, they will be able to direct their minds to the point should it assume any relevance, which it doesn't seem to have at the moment.'

'You might feel differently if she had been *your* daughter, sir.'

'That observation is bordering on the impertinent,' Mr. Kerslake said coldly, at the same time casting a reproving look at one of the male jurors who was vigorously nodding his head in apparent sympathy with Andrews.

'I apologise sir,' Andrews said stiffly, and sat down.

P.C. Newbold was the next witness and testified to finding Susan's body.

'Have you any suggestions as to what happened to her shoes?' Mr. Denny asked.

'No, sir.'

'Has a thorough search been made for them?'

'Yes, sir. With dogs.'

'And they've never been found?'

'No, sir.'

'Would you care to speculate on their disappearance?'

'No, sir,' Newbold replied firmly, at the same moment as Mr. Kerslake voiced his objection to the question.

'The witness is here to testify the facts, not speculate about them.'

'I'm well aware of that,' Mr. Denny replied unabashed—and sat down.

The two witnesses who followed were the manager and waiter from the Yellow Caravan. Their evidence created an atmosphere in which Kingston became the target of almost palpable indignation and silent revilement. Sitting immediately behind his solicitor with arms folded across his chest, he stared fixedly to his front. Manton wondered whether he had been warned not to shuffle or squirm in his seat whatever disagreeable shocks the evidence might produce.

Mr. Denny's questioning of these two witnesses was angled to show that Susan

225

Andrews and his client were an ordinary couple enjoying an innocent evening together, and that no one could have detected signs of overt lust on the part of his client, since such were non-existent.

Andrews didn't question either witness and Manton presumed that he was content to identify himself with Mr. Denny's line. After all, his main concern seemed to be to prove his daughter innocent of any charge of sexual precocity—and this had been a by-product of Mr. Denny's own questions.

There followed the evidence of Captain Armstrong on which Mr. Denny quickly fastened in order to underline its favourable aspects to his client as to the time Susan had last been seen alive. Over an hour after Kingston had left her, he pointed out to the jury.

'Over an hour after *he says* that he left her, don't you mean.' Mr. Kerslake remarked.

'When Mr. Crowland gives evidence he'll prove that what my client says is the truth,' Mr. Denny snapped.

'The evidence of the gentleman you refer to has no bearing on how this girl met her death and I'm not proposing to call him,' Mr. Kerslake said serenely.

For a second Mr. Denny looked aghast. Then eyes flashing angrily, he said, 'It will be very unfair to my client if you don't. It could result in a denial of justice, and it would certainly indicate a disinclination on your part to probe as deeply as the circumstances require.'

'I propose to conduct this inquest in my own way, Mr. Denny, and not even your—your persuasive tongue will induce me to call evidence which I regard as immaterial. However, should it seem to acquire a certain relevance between now and the termination of these proceedings, I shall of course be prepared to reconsider the matter.' He consulted his watch. 'We will now have a fifteen-minute adjournment.'

Manton watched Mr. Thirkell shuffle the sheets of foolscap on which he had been making copious notes. He wished he knew why Lady Neale had considered it necessary to have her solicitor attend the inquest. Was it merely because there might be an oblique reference to her son having enjoyed a chequered friendship with the dead girl, or did she have reason to fear that something more sinister might emerge, something of which Manton had no present knowledge? He decided to try to find out.

'You're very much the silent witness in our midst,' he said with a friendly smile.

Mr. Thirkell looked up and grinned. 'I shall have to try to find at least one question to ask before the end.'

'You'll have your chance when Kingston's in the box.'

The young solicitor pursed his lips. 'I hope

not. Frankly, I don't relish getting drawn into the fray. I'd sooner remain on the touchline. I mean, it could all be a bit tricky and embarrassing.'

'In what way?'

'Well, Lady Neale doesn't want her son's name mixed up in such an unsavoury affair.'

'Is that all she's worried about?'

'What do you mean?'

'Are you sure she's not worried about something more sinister than mere mention of his name?'

Mr. Thirkell looked startled. 'Good heavens, you're not trying to suggest that Michael Neale had anything to do with the girl's death?'

'I was just wondering whether that mightn't be Lady Neale's major concern.'

Mr. Thirkell suddenly blushed hard. 'Really, I don't think we should continue this discussion.'

The matter was, in any event, taken out of their hands by the return of Mr. Kerslake, refreshed, as Manton later learnt, by a cup of coffee brewed specially for him by Mrs. Newbold and brought to court by her husband.

'I now call Bernard Kingston,' Mr. Kerslake said in a clear voice.

Kingston rose from his seat, squared his shoulders and stepped across to the witness-box. He took the oath in a ringing tone and nervously fingered his tie.

'The jury won't like that,' Avis whispered into Manton's ear.

'What?'

'His wearing a black tie. It strikes a false note, like wearing a lily in your button-hole at the boss's funeral.'

After warning the witness that he was not obliged to answer any questions which might incriminate him, Mr. Kerslake proceeded to lead his evidence, recording without comment its gloss of self-justifying innocence. It seemed to Manton that he had decided in connection with this witness to see if others would do his work for him. Moreover, it was clear that he had taken particular pleasure in depriving Mr. Denny of any opportunity of legitimate objection.

'Are there any questions you wish to put to your client?' he asked, laying down his fountain pen and gently rubbing the fingers of his right hand.

'Most certainly,' Mr. Denny replied, springing to his feet with ill-concealed impatience.

'Is it a fact, Mr. Kingston, that you have volunteered to give evidence at this inquest?'

'It is.'

'And that you have made no attempt to evade any questions on the grounds of self-incrimination?'

'I have not.'

'Have you anything to hide?'

'Nothing.'

'Have you told this court the whole truth?'

'I have.'

'And do you swear . . .'

'He has taken the oath,' Mr. Kerslake broke in. 'There's no need for any further swearing, forensic, rhetorical or otherwise.'

Mr. Denny affected not to have heard the interruption. 'And is it the absolute truth that you had nothing to do with Susan Andrews's death?'

'I swear it.'

Mr. Kerslake let out a theatrical sigh as Mr. Denny went on, 'And have you made some inquiries yourself into this matter?'

'Yes.'

'And what have you found out?'

'That Susan had a regular boy-friend.'

'I won't ask you to mention his name in open court for the time being,' Mr. Denny intervened quickly, casting a glance of dislike in the direction of Mr. Thirkell and Manton, 'But was this boy-friend you refer to in Offing on the evening of her death?'

'I understand so.'

'And have you been able to discover whether *he* might have had a motive for murdering her?'

At this point, Mr. Thirkell began to flash looks of alarm at Mr. Kerslake, who daintily moistened his lips and turning to Kingston said:

'I rule that question inadmissible, so don't answer it.'

'In my submission it's perfectly admissible,' Mr. Denny said hotly.

'I have ruled to the contrary. It's inviting speculation; moreover, it's immaterial.'

'How can it be immaterial if it goes to show who may have killed Susan?'

'I have given my ruling,' Mr. Kerslake replied in a tone of such authority that even Mr. Denny was obliged to acquiesce.

'I have no further questions to ask in view of your attitude,' he said.

Mr. Thirkell pulled out his handkerchief and dabbed at his forehead in obvious relief.

'No questions, sir,' he said with a courteous inclination of his head.

All eyes turned on George Andrews as he stood up and stared at Kingston across the small court-room with patent hostility.

'You intended to seduce my daughter, didn't you?'

'Certainly not.'

'Have you lied to the police?'

'I object to that question,' Mr. Denny snapped. 'It lacks any precision.'

Mr. Kerslake ignored him. 'Well, have you lied to the police at any time since this inquiry began?'

'I think the police are satisfied with the answers I've given to their questions,' Kingston said defiantly. 'Otherwise I assume that they would have arrested me.'

An audible gasp rippled through the court. That their quarry should admit the peril of his predicament so boldly!

'Do you still say that you dropped my daughter a hundred yards from home at around half-past ten?'

'I do.'

'Then what was she doing out by Langdale Farm over two miles away an hour later?'

Mr. Denny sprang up. 'That's not a question for the witness to answer.'

'I'm sorry, sir,' Andrews said with heavy sarcasm, 'but I don't enjoy Mr. Denny's advantage of being a solicitor.'

'I understand you were a police officer for several years, so you should have some knowledge of the rules of evidence.'

'Kindly cease this altercation,' Mr. Kerslake managed to say at last. 'Have you any further questions, Mr. Andrews?'

Andrews slowly brought his gaze back to the witness. 'In the presence of the jury, I put it to you, Mr. Kingston, that you murdered my daughter.'

The hubbub evoked by the question was such that it was a full minute before complete silence was restored. Then in an equally challenging tone, Kingston replied, 'That's a ridiculous and quite fantastic suggestion.'

'Any further questions?' Mr. Kerslake asked again.

'I'd like to put a question.' It was one of the jurors who spoke, a large, red-faced, family-looking man.

'Very well,' Mr. Kerslake conceded doubtfully.

'If this was such an innocent evening, why did you drop the girl some distance from her home? Why didn't you take her to her front door?'

A number of other jurors nodded their heads in approving silence. Kingston looked at them nonplussed for several seconds.

'Because even though it was an entirely innocent evening, I realised it might be open to misconstruction.'

'I'll say,' the juror observed audibly, turning to his neighbour.

With a small bow to the coroner, Kingston left the witness-box and returned to his seat to enter into an immediate whispered colloquy with Mr. Denny, a defiant attempt, Manton surmised, to present a solid front in the face of a roomful of latent hostility.

Mr. Kerslake who had been studying his list of witnesses now looked up and said in a tone which managed to convey all previous unawareness of such a name, 'Call Simon Manton.'

Manton took the oath in the nicely-judged

tone of quiet sincerity which most detectives learn to acquire, and laid his notebook on the ledge in front of him. As he did so, he saw Avis come hurrying into court and then stop with a look of dismay when he observed Manton in the box. It was the expression of a traveller who arrives in time to see the tail light of the train disappearing when he was certain he had several minutes in hand. For a second he stood mouthing at Manton, who watched him with baffled helplessness, then with a despairing gesture he sat down in Manton's seat and began scribbling on a piece of paper.

Mr. Kerslake who had been reading through the statement which Manton had supplied to him had not been a spectator of the fruitless mime which had taken place, and by the time he was ready to start, Avis had departed as dramatically as he had arrived.

Slowly, and with great care, the coroner led Manton through the history of his inquiries into Susan's death. When he reached the end he turned and asked with great deliberation, 'And despite all efforts, is it a fact that you and those whose advice you have sought have not considered that there was sufficient evidence to justify an arrest?'

It sounded as though Mr. Kerslake was proposing to ride his jury off any verdict naming Kingston as the murderer. It remained to be seen, however, how successful he would be. George Andrews certainly had one staunch ally amongst them, a fairly vocal one too, it seemed, who might well use his own persuasive powers against the coroner's more cautious approach when it came to reaching a verdict.

'That is so, sir,' Manton replied and caught sight out of the corner of his eye of at least two jurors shaking their heads in stony disapproval. He shifted slightly to face Mr. Denny as he rose like a rocket from its launching pad.

'And I take it,' he said grimly, 'that it's not through any finer feelings toward anyone that an arrest has not been made, by which I mean that only lack of evidence and nothing else has held you back?'

'Correct.'

'And just so that the jury may know, would you tell us whose advice you have sought in this matter?'

'The Director of Public Prosecutions.'

'And who else?'

'I've naturally consulted my own superiors as well.'

'The Chief Constable of the County for example?'

'Yes.'

'And the Commissioner of Police for the Metropolis?'

'The Assistant Commissioner.'

Mr. Denny nodded with stern satisfaction. 'And so we may assume that not one of those eminent gentleman regard the evidence you've been able to accumulate as sufficient to support a charge of murder against any named individual?'

Manton lowered his eyes and there was several seconds silence as he pondered his reply. He was greatly tempted to retort that the Chief Constable had been all for arresting Mr. Denny's client, but he knew that this would bring him short-lived satisfaction and that the subsequent rumpus would damage him more than it would anyone else.

'What you may assume, sir, is that the evidence has not been considered sufficient to justify an arrest. I obviously can't divulge details of conferences which have been held to discuss the case.' He hoped he had managed to answer Mr. Denny's question and at the same time indicate to the jury that if *they* cared to name Kingston in their verdict, good luck to them since he, Manton, wouldn't feel aggrieved.

Wisely, however, Mr. Denny now changed tack, apparently realising that any attempt to use Manton as an instrument for white-washing his client was hardly likely to achieve that end.

'Tell me, Superintendent,' he said in his nearest approach to a silky tone, 'how many suspects have you investigated in the course of your inquiries?'

'I don't think I can answer that.'

'You mean you won't answer it?'

'He said "can't",' Mr. Kerslake broke in.

'I know he did, but since that is obviously an untruthful as well as an unintelligent answer, I was giving him the benefit of interpreting it as wilful rather than stupid.' He fixed Manton with a look of dislike. 'I'll repeat my question, how many suspects have there been in this case?'

'It depends what you mean by suspect.'

Mr. Denny's eyes flashed angrily. 'Don't fence with me, Superintendent. You know quite well what I mean and I want an answer to my question.'

'Well, *I* don't know what you mean,' Mr. Kerslake said. 'Suspect is a subjective term. You might receive different answers from different people connected with the case. This officer, for example, might say that at one time he suspected the whole male population of the village, whereas another might say that he never considered there was ever more than one suspect.'

Turning back to Manton, Mr. Denny said in a venomous tone, 'Let me try and rephrase my question so as to avoid further sophistry on the use of a plain English word.' He flung out a hand at Kingston. 'It's a fact, isn't it, that Mr. Kingston, here, is a suspect?'

'Yes.'

'So you do know what the word means! Who

else apart from Mr. Kingston came under suspicion?'

'Quite a number of people were eliminated in the course of normal inquiries,' Manton replied uncomfortably. He reckoned this answer was not too far removed from truth to be capable of justification. After all, it had been part of routine to eliminate Andrews himself, not to mention all the boys of the village Susan had ever known. Admittedly, none of them had ever been serious suspects but that didn't mean that the usual steps hadn't been taken formally to eliminate them. In the end, of course, only Kingston and young Neale had remained.

'Are you quite certain that there isn't somebody apart from my client at whom the finger of suspicion still points?'

'It points most strongly at your client.'

'I didn't ask you that,' Mr. Denny snarled. 'Does it point anywhere else at all?' When Manton hesitated, he added, 'Remember you're on oath, Superintendent.'

Manton flushed. 'I don't need to be reminded of that, sir, but I'm afraid your questions require rather careful answering.' Because you're such a tricky little runt, he would have liked to have added.

'I'm tired of beating about the bush, Superintendent,' Mr. Denny exploded as Manton was about to reply. 'Just answer me this, does the name Michael Neale mean anything to you?'

'Silence!' roared the coroner's officer at the eruption of excited murmurs which broke out all over the court.

'Yes.'

'He was a friend of Susan Andrews, wasn't he?'

'I understand so.'

'Has he ever come under suspicion?'

Mr. Thirkell who had been silently gobbling like a turkey now rose uneasily to his feet.

'I object,' he said.

'And I demand an answer to my question,' Mr. Denny snapped back.

Mr. Kerslake, who seemed to have lost temporary control over the proceedings, reasserted himself. 'Since Mr. Denny has seen fit to mention this name'—his tone conveyed all he felt about Mr. Denny—'perhaps you had better answer the question, Officer.'

'The person you mention was one of several whose movements on the night of the murder have been checked by the police.'

'Has he been cleared?'

'I object,' Mr. Thirkell said again, though this time more boldly.

'I uphold the objection,' Mr. Kerslake added quickly.

'Since there is an apparent conspiracy to conceal all the facts, I can only draw my own conclusions and, if necessary, seek my remedy

239

elsewhere.' With this Parthian shot, Mr. Denny sat down, not unpleased with the scene of disarray his questions had provoked.

Manton, however, found himself suddenly more interested in the note which Avis had left for him and which lay folded neatly on top of his papers than he was in answering a lot of tiresome questions from people with axes to grind. He gave an inward groan as Mr. Thirkell pulled himself to his feet and in an anxious voice asked: 'Would it be right to say that you have absolutely no evidence to show that Mr. Neale had anything to do with this crime?'

'There is no evidence connecting him with it.'

'Thank you,' Mr. Thirkell said with obvious relief and sat down.

Manton's eye fell again on the tantalising note which awaited his release from the witness-box, but this was not yet to be for Andrews now stood up. Studying a piece of paper in his hand, he asked, 'Would you agree that the following points indicate Kingston as the murderer of my daughter?'

Mr. Denny leapt up as though a charge of dynamite had been exploded beneath him. 'That's a monstrously improper question and I ask you to rule it out of order.'

'On what grounds?' Mr. Kerslake inquired with quiet malice.

'It is not for this witness to indicate any such

thing. It's a matter for the jury to decide when they've heard all the facts.'

'Yes, I can't allow that question, Mr. Andrews.'

'I hope that you will allow me to address the jury,' George Andrews said doggedly.

Mr. Kerslake glanced swiftly at Mr. Denny to observe his reaction, but for once there didn't appear to be any.

'I'll give you my decision when the time arrives. Meanwhile, have you any questions for this witness?'

Andrews consulted the piece of paper in his hand. 'Have you tried to trace the murderer through the piece of towel thread found between Susan's teeth?'

'Yes, but without success I'm afraid.'

'And her shoes?'

'I only wish we could find them, then we might know why they were removed.'

'So whatever verdict is returned in this court, your inquiries will still continue?'

'Very much so.'

Andrews sat down and Mr. Kerslake, after looking at his watch, announced, 'The Court will now adjourn till half-past two.'

Three strides brought Manton to the note which Avis had left and which had been taunting him for the past hour. With eager fingers he opened it and read:

'I think Susan's shoes have been found.'

CHAPTER TWENTY-SIX

When Manton reached the police station there was a message to the effect that Avis had gone out to the scene of recovery which was in the vicinity of Offing airfield. Manton was about to go after him when Avis returned carrying a polythene bag in which two muddy objects could be seen.

'I think these are Susan's all right, sir,' he said excitedly. 'But Andrews will be able to confirm it.'

'Tell me everything,' Manton said impatiently. 'I've been burning with curiosity since you popped in and out of court like an anxious hamster.'

Avis grinned boyishly. 'I didn't think you'd be in the box till this afternoon. I don't know if you remember, sir, there's a ploughed field about two hundred yards east of where Susan's body was found.' Manton nodded. 'Well, the farmer who owns it is erecting a barn in the corner nearest the airfield and this morning one of those excavating machines arrived to start levelling it off. With the third mouthful of earth it seized, it dug up a pair of shoes. The fellow who was operating it is a local lad and of course he knew it was near there that Susan's body had been found and that her shoes were missing so he immediately sent a message down to the station. I went off there as soon as I'd written you that note.'

'Any obvious reason why they haven't been found before?' Manton asked suspiciously.

'They were buried about two feet down, and as the field had been recently ploughed anyway, there was no particular indication of digging. It wasn't like somebody having dug a hole in the middle of a lawn.'

Manton put a hand inside the polythene bag and gently extracted the shoes. They were heavily caked in mud and it was impossible to detect anything apart from the fact that they *were* a pair of shoes. Female shoes with stiletto heels. A call was put through to George Andrews, and ten minutes later he arrived at the station.

'Yes, those are Susan's all right,' he said. 'Where'd you find them?'

Avis told him.

Manton said, 'I better have a word with the coroner and ask him to adjourn the inquest until the lab. has reported. Meanwhile, Dick, you'd better hop into a car and get down to the laboratory as fast as four wheels will take you. And impress on everyone the need for secrecy.'

'I've already threatened the chap who found them with slow death if he talks.'

Mr. Kerslake received Manton's information with a characteristic air of detachment. 'I assume, Superintendent, that you would prefer the reason for the adjournment not to be mentioned in court.'

'I would, sir. News of what's happened is bound to get around sooner or later, but the later it happens the better for me.' He sighed. 'If only I can keep it quiet until Mr. Champigny has made his examination.'

The general expectation had been that the afternoon would be taken up with a few remaining witnesses, and if time permitted, the coroner's summing-up. But when, soon after three o'clock, the last witness left the box and Mr. Denny rose importantly to his feet, Mr. Kerslake looked at him with a sardonic expression and said, 'Yes, Mr. Denny?'

'I wish to address you, sir.'

Mr. Kerslake shook his head. 'I'm adjourning this inquest till one week today.'

Mr. Denny looked about him in bewilderment. 'But this is most inconvenient,' he expostulated, but Mr. Kerslake had already disappeared through the door into his private room.

'You'd better speak to Manton if you want to know what's going on,' Sankey observed, coming up beside Mr. Denny. 'He was closeted with the coroner for five minutes before the resumption this afternoon. Slipped in and out by the back way. I just happened to catch sight of him sneaking round there.'

'Oh, indeed!' Mr. Denny remarked ominously, only to find that Manton, too, had disappeared by the time he turned his head.

And when he looked back Sankey had also melted away again. He was on his way to a call-box to phone through his story to the paper. If he could obtain confirmation of the rumour he'd picked up that Susan's shoes had been found, they could have that as a nice little bonus for the stop-press. He must go and see Andrews. It was significant that he hadn't put in an appearance at court in the afternoon.

★   ★   ★

Peggy Kingston had just sent her daughters up to bed and was wondering whether she could be bothered to get herself any supper when she heard the fumbling of a key in the front-door. She went out into the hall in time to see her husband lurch into the house. He paused and blinked as though surprised by her presence.

'I'm drunk, Peggy,' he said thickly.

'You'd better come and sit in the kitchen. You don't want the children to hear you.'

'That's right.' He nodded and followed her meekly into the kitchen and flopped down on a chair while she closed the door. 'I'm sorry I'm drunk, Peggy, but anyone would go out and get sloshed after the day I've had.'

'Is the inquest over?'

'No.'

'Does it continue tomorrow?'

'Next week.'

'Was Mr. Denny good?'

'I'll say! He tied 'em all in knots.' He paused and a tear trickled down his cheek. 'But they're after me, Peggy. They're all after me. They think I did it and they want to see me hanged.' His voice rose on a note of self-pity. 'It was terrible sitting there all day feeling their hatred and realising they're all determined to get me arrested.' He put out a hand. 'You must help me, Peggy; you're my wife and I've got no one else.'

'I expect you're exaggerating, but we'll go and see Mr. Denny in the morning if you like.'

'I'm frightened, Peggy, I'm really frightened. That was why I went and got drunk.'

'What are you frightened about?'

'The police have discovered something fresh, that's why it's been adjourned. They are going to try to break me down. It's all part of their war of nerves.'

Peggy Kingston sighed. 'If you're innocent, what have you to worry about?'

'But I am innocent and yet look what they're doing to me. They're certain I murdered her and they're going to frame me.'

'The police don't behave like that in this

country.'

He gave a mocking laugh which turned into a paroxysm of coughing. When he had recovered, he looked at his wife with bloodshot eyes and said slowly, 'I think you'd believe me if I told you I had murdered that girl.'

★　　　★　　　★

Michael Neale bought a copy of an evening paper and took it back to his room. It carried a full account of the inquest, and he flung himself into a comfortable chair and swung his legs over the side as he settled down to read it. He glanced first at the end in the hope of seeing that the jury had returned a verdict against Kingston and that Susan's death was shortly to be vindicated, but he gave a small frown of annoyance when he read that the inquest had been adjourned for a week. He tilted back his head and stared up at the ceiling as slowly a tender smile replaced the frown.

'It's all right, darling,' he murmured. 'Be patient, for I give you my promise that your death is going to be avenged. If the law fails, I shall take over from the law.'

He blinked away the tears which pricked his eyes each time he thought of Susan, and lifted a hand to pick the newspaper off his stomach. As he did so his attention was caught by the stop-press item and his sad, dreamy expression abruptly vanished as he read about the recovery of the shoes. Its place was taken by a look of thoughtful cunning.

*   *   *

It was shortly after nine o'clock that evening when Avis phoned from the Yard.

'Sorry about the delay, sir, but Mr. Champigny went off to another court this afternoon and didn't return till nearly six, and everyone else was either out or too tied up with their own work.'

'That's O.K., but what's the answer?' Manton asked impatiently. Although Avis was not given to prolixity, Manton had observed before that he was inclined to embark on lengthy explanations when these could well wait.

'Well, that's the odd thing, sir, there doesn't appear to be anything wrong with the shoes apart from some oil stains. There are a few on each, but otherwise as far as Mr. Champigny can see there aren't any significant marks on either their insides or their outsides. I can't think why whoever it was removed them, unless it was part of a fetish.'

While Avis had been speaking, Manton had been staring at the wall with his eyes screwed up in concentrated thought.

'Anything else you want me to do here, sir,

before I come back?'

'No, I'll expect you in about an hour Dick. And by then I'll have had time to check on something.'

'Something to do with the shoes, sir?' Avis asked, with sudden curiosity.

'Yes. I want to confirm my recollection of a passing remark somebody made to us early on in the inquiry. I'll tell you about it when you get back.'

No lights were showing from the Thrupps' home when Manton drew up outside, but he trusted this meant only that they were clustered round the television set in the kitchen at the rear. It apparently did, since he hadn't long to wait before there were sounds of bolts and chains being unfastened and Thrupp himself appeared in the doorway.

'Is Christine in?'

'She's doing her homework.'

'I shan't keep her a couple of minutes.'

'I thought I told you I didn't want her dragged into this,' Thrupp said in a truculent voice.

'I managed to keep her out of the inquest, didn't I?' Manton replied quickly. At this moment it didn't matter that it was the coroner who had gratuitously omitted her from the list of witnesses, he was going to claim the credit.

Thrupp turned back into the house muttering to himself. Manton thought he caught the words, 'worse than the Gestapo'. A few seconds later, Christine appeared eating a banana.

'Hallo,' she said, in a noncommittal tone.

'Do you remember telling me the first time I saw you something about Susan not wearing her good shoes when she went out with Michael Neale?'

Christine nodded. 'She said his car was all dirty round the floor and used to mess them up. And he used to tell her that it was her fault because her heels dug holes in his mat.'

'Thank you very much, Christine. That's all.'

She looked at him in surprise, then said, 'You didn't tell my dad that I let you into the house the other week, did you?'

'No.'

'Good night, then.'

Manton returned to the station without delay and put through an immediate call to Neale's college, where he was connected with the porter's lodge.

'I should like to speak to Mr. Michael Neale, please.'

''Fraid you can't. I saw him go out not five minutes ago. Want to leave a message?'

'No, thanks.'

Manton rang off. He knew he must make a decision—and quickly.

CHAPTER TWENTY-SEVEN

Manton was to wonder later what the course of events might have been if he had not taken the decision immediately to send out an alert for Neale, and where that young man might have got to if he hadn't been politely stopped as he was driving out of the garage where he kept his car and invited to go along to the local station to await Manton's arrival.

It was between eleven and half-past before the officers reached Cambridge and found Neale sitting apparently at ease in a cheerless interview room with a half-drunk cup of tea beside him. He looked up as Manton and Avis entered and eyed them with quiet reserve.

'Do you know why you're here?' Manton asked.

'Because I was told you wished to see me urgently. Incidentally, I have to be in college by midnight.'

'Do you know the reason I want to see you?'

'I don't think so,' Neale said in a calm, unruffled tone.

'Susan Andrews's shoes have been found, dug up from where someone buried them.'

'I saw that in this evening's paper.'

'Did you bury them?'

Neale looked at them with a shyly mocking

smile. 'You must have some reason for asking such an extraordinary question.'

'I have. The shoes were covered with oil stains, which I believe came from your car.'

'Oh?'

'Christine Thrupp has told us that Susan wouldn't wear her best shoes when she was going in your car for that very reason: because they used to get stained with oil. That's true, isn't it?'

Neale gave a faint shrug as if to indicate that the interview was already becoming tedious. 'Yes, she did complain once or twice and I used to tell her it was her fault for wearing shoes with spikes for heels which dug holes in the mat.'

'Yes, I heard that too.'

'Well, that's all there was to it. We didn't even quarrel about it.' He looked at his watch and made a slight face. 'Much more?'

Manton nodded. 'Possibly several hours.'

'But the college . . .'

'You'll have to trust me to straighten things out with your college authorities in due course.'

Neale slowly licked his lips and Manton observed a slight glistening of his forehead. His general air, however, was still one of sleepy calm.

'I now ask you again, was it you who buried Susan's shoes?'

There was a full minute's silence during which Neale stared impassively at various points in the room. Only a slight contraction of his eyes indicated that he had heard the question and was pondering an answer.

'No,' he said at length.

'It took you a very long time to answer that simple question.'

Neale shrugged. 'It's you who has said the interview may last several hours.'

'Supposing I tell you that the oil stains on Susan's shoes can be proved to have come from your car?' To be sure Manton hoped that this might prove to be possible, though it wasn't so at the present moment. But interviews of this sort had much in common with a game of poker. The person holding the stronger hand usually won, but it was not invariable.

Neale passed his tongue over his lips again, then said slowly, 'It doesn't follow that the person who buried the shoes was also responsible for Susan's death.'

'Agreed,' Manton said quickly, with a sudden rising of hope. 'Were you responsible for her death?'

Neale shook his head emphatically. 'No, that saloon-bar gigolo Kingston was.'

Manton stared at him with a puzzled frown. There was something unreal about his dreamily withdrawn air. He might almost have willed himself into a state of trance.

'Why do you say that Kingston was responsible for her death?' he asked in a curious tone.

'He took her out and tried to debauch her. He per—'

'Yes?'

'Nothing.'

'Were you going to say that he perverted her?' Neale shrugged impatiently. 'That he turned her head?'

This time he looked up sharply. 'Sometimes Susan needed protecting from herself, but he was just out to use her.'

'And that's why you say he was responsible for her death?'

'Of course.'

There was a pause and Manton said quietly, 'But it was you who killed her, wasn't it?'

Neale's face took on a sudden waxiness, his eyes were filled with a look of sick horror, and his lips quivered.

'It was the last thing I wanted to do,' he said hoarsely. 'I loved her. She never understood how much I loved her. She taunted me, she didn't know what she was saying. She'd been unnerved by Kingston's behaviour, neither of us was in our proper mind that evening.'

He stopped abruptly and, looking at Manton with a distraught expression, let out a shuddering groan.

'Hadn't you better tell me the whole story?' Manton said quietly. 'Though you don't have to if you don't wish to.' He glanced at Avis to make sure he was ready to take down what Neale might say.

Neale passed a hand wearily across his forehead. He gave the appearance of someone suffering from shock, part of whose mental processes were feathering like a runaway propeller. In a far-away voice he said, 'It had been arranged, ages before, that I should come home that Friday and take her up to a party in London, the one I told you about. I was to pick her up on the outskirts of the village—we could never meet openly—but she didn't turn up. I waited over an hour and then drove up to London alone. But I didn't stay there long; I couldn't, I wasn't in the mood. And then when I got back to Offing I parked the car near her home and walked down the lane to their cottage. I could see the landing light was on and knew she must be out because her parents always left it on if she wasn't home. So I went back to my car and waited at the top of the lane. I must have been there over an hour, I know it was after midnight when I suddenly saw her. She was walking or rather staggering along the road. I ran over to her, but she was too upset even to be surprised at seeing me there. She was dishevelled and she'd been crying, and I made her come and sit in the car. It was some time before she could tell me what had happened but gradually I got the whole story from her.' He closed his eyes as though with a sudden stab of pain. Then opening them again, he went on, 'On the way back from the Yellow Caravan, the swine had tried to interfere with her and there'd been a bit of a struggle in the car. That's when a button got torn off her blouse. When she refused to let him do anything, he shoved her out of the car and told her that little girls who weren't prepared to pay for their supper could jolly well walk home. She was over two miles from Offing and she had to walk the whole way back.'

'That's when Captain Armstrong must have seen her,' Avis murmured. Manton nodded.

'What happened next?' he asked.

'I drove her around for a while trying to calm her down and then I went and parked up on the airfield. We often used to go up there. I tried to kiss her but she pushed me away and said . . . said things she didn't mean. Spiteful things.' His expression became anguished.

'What did she say?' Manton asked quietly.

'She said I was like a fumbling schoolboy and that at least Kingston had been a man. She taunted me about the time I had tried to have intercourse with her. It had been her idea, but I . . . it didn't work and she was upset. We never tried again. She was being deliberately hurtful and I lost my temper with her. Suddenly all I wanted to do was to hurt her too, except that I didn't really. I remember getting hold of her scarf and pulling it, and then the next thing was she had flopped against me. I couldn't believe she was dead, I was petrified. Eventually I lifted her out and laid her in the ditch. She must have been scraping her feet on the car floor because I saw that her shoes were all oily, so I took them off and buried them in the field. Then I drove straight home.' He paused exhausted and took a gulp of cold, greasy tea.

'Were you prepared to let Kingston go to prison for the crime you committed?' Manton asked.

'I wouldn't have minded. It was he who really killed Susan, none of this would have happened but for him. If you'd seen her that night as I did, you'd understand. You'd realise that he's guiltier than I am.' He sighed wearily. 'But now that it's all over, I don't care any more, you can do what you like with me.'

'Did you put a towel over her head when you were strangling her?' Manton asked with sudden recollection.

Neale gave an uninterested shake of the head. 'No.'

'A piece of cotton was found between two of Susan's teeth . . .'

With an apparent effort Neale brought his mind back to what Manton was saying.

'I think it came from my shirt. I was wearing one of those towelled shirts and . . . and when she was struggling she tried to bite me.'

'A towelled shirt!' Manton murmured in

257

dawning comprehension. He glanced at his watch. One-thirty a.m. He supposed he must begin doing some telephoning. At least the lines should be clear.

'Stay with him, Dick,' he said, as he rose and stretched his aching limbs. He felt little sense of satisfaction, merely the physical soreness of exhaustion.

Michael Neale didn't stir as Manton left the room. He was leaning back with his eyes closed, and his breathing so shallow that he could have been mistaken for dead.

CHAPTER TWENTY-EIGHT

Six weeks had gone by and it was an oppressive afternoon at the end of July. A few minutes before, the Assize Court had been packed to its ancient ceiling, but now only Manton and Avis remained, scooping together their scattered papers.

When the end had come, Michael Neale had been the first to depart, to the cells below. Then the judge had made his final bows and melted through the heavily curtained door at the back of the bench. Thereafter, counsel, Press and public had swarmed out leaving behind them an atmosphere of stale, dusty melancholy.

'I reckon he was pretty lucky,' Avis remarked

as he bent down to rescue a document from the floor.

'I thought he'd get away with manslaughter,' Manton said.

'Even so, three years is a lenient sentence. I must say his counsel didn't half pile it on about the girl.' He gave a resigned shrug. 'Personally, I think Neale's a bit bats.'

Manton looked thoughtful. 'They could probably have run diminished responsibility if they'd wanted. It wouldn't have been difficult to find a psychiatrist or two who was prepared to say he was suffering from an abnormality of the mind, et cetera. On the other hand, if they'd got a manslaughter verdict on that ground, he'd almost certainly have received a longer sentence. On the whole, provocation was probably the best defence.' He smiled wryly. 'Well, it was, wasn't it?'

They made their way out into the empty corridor where Manton paused and wrinkled his nose with distaste.

'I don't know about you, Dick, but I shan't mind if I never see Offing again.'

★　　★　　★

Bernard Kingston strode confidently into the saloon bar of the Nag's Head. He was pleased to note that it was empty apart from a couple at a table in the corner.

'Hi, there, precious,' he called out to the barmaid, whose back he could see through a doorway. She turned and her features broke into a warm smile.

'Hello, dear,' she said, approaching with the walk she reserved for most favoured customers. 'All over, is it?'

'Yes, thank God! Give me a double Scotch, sweetheart. And what'll yours be?'

'I'll have a Scotch too, thanks.'

He watched her with approving eyes as she moved away to deal with the order. Nice legs, cosy figure; and that walk of hers was definitely exciting. He reckoned she must be in the early thirties and an experienced woman if ever he'd seen one. What a lucky chance it was that he'd happened to drop in the previous day on his way home from court. It looked as though further visits would be worth the detour. She brought the drinks and they toasted each other.

'What time are you free in the evenings?' he asked with a sly wink.

*   *   *

George Andrews laid down his knife and fork and pushed his plate from him.

'Aren't you hungry?' his wife asked.

He shook his head. 'No, I don't feel like food this evening.' With a sudden burst of bitterness he went on, 'Three years, that's all he got!

Three years for strangling Susan!'

'There's nothing more you can do about it, dear,' Winnie Andrews said with resignation. 'It's all over now. No point in banging your head against a wall.'

'You wouldn't talk like that if you'd been in court and heard the way defence counsel blackened her character. Why, even the judge as good as suggested to the jury that she was nothing better than the village trollop.' He clenched his fist. 'I'm not taking that. I'll fight and go on fighting till her name is cleared, even if it does mean, as you put it, banging my head against a wall. Anyway, none of them knew Susan.'

His wife sighed. 'I sometimes wonder,' she said wistfully, 'how well *we* really knew her.'

›› If you've enjoyed this book and would like to discover more great vintage crime and thriller titles, as well as the most exciting crime and thriller authors writing today, visit: ››

The Murder Room
Where Criminal Minds Meet

themurderroom.com

www.ingramcontent.com/pod-product-compliance
Ingram Content Group UK Ltd.
Pitfield, Milton Keynes, MK11 3LW, UK
UKHW040434280225
455666UK00003B/66